Racing Hearts

New York Times Bestselling Author

Vicki Lewis Thompson

Nancy Warren ♥ Dorien Kelly

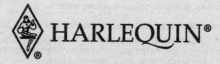

HARLEQUIN®

TORONTO • NEW YORK • LONDON
AMSTERDAM • PARIS • SYDNEY • HAMBURG
STOCKHOLM • ATHENS • TOKYO • MILAN • MADRID
PRAGUE • WARSAW • BUDAPEST • AUCKLAND

Recycling programs
for this product may
not exist in your area.

ISBN-13: 978-0-373-83740-3

RACING HEARTS

Copyright © 2010 by Harlequin Books S.A.

The publisher acknowledges the copyright holders
of the individual works as follows:

A CALCULATED RISK
Copyright © 2010 by Vicki Lewis Thompson

AN OUTSIDE CHANCE
Copyright © 2010 by Nancy Warren

THIS TIME AROUND
Copyright © 2010 by Dorien Kelly

CONTENTS

For Mary Jo LaBeff for sharing
her love of NASCAR and her precious
photos of Daytona.
Her enthusiastic support added energy
and laughter to this project.

A CALCULATED RISK
Vicki Lewis Thompson

Dear Reader,

I'm a NASCAR convert. I confess that until diving into this story, I knew very little about NASCAR. But as the proud owner of a hot little two-seater sports car, I was more than willing to learn about fast cars and the daredevils who drive them.

Am I glad I did! I bought videos, pestered friends, researched online and bought *NASCAR for Dummies* by the intrepid Mark Martin. I was in total immersion mode. I couldn't quite fit in a trip to Daytona for research, so I did the next best thing and looked for the biggest, baddest flat screen I could find, which turned out to be at my local sports bar.

And now I get it! I understand why men cheer and women swoon. This is one fascinating sport packed with thrills, chills and...in the case of Roni and Judd, the perfect environment for a budding romance. NASCAR rocks!

Speedily yours,

Vicki Lewis Thompson

CHAPTER ONE

"Ow!" RONI THREW THE mascara wand into the hotel-room sink and grabbed a tissue. Holding it to her watering eye, she used all her favorite four-letter words. At the race track she was considered a mechanical genius, so why couldn't she manage to apply mascara without stabbing herself in the eye?

Once her eye stopped watering, she took a deep breath and surveyed the damage. Yuck. Bloodshot was not the look she was going for. Served her right for waiting until the last minute to present crew chief Judd Timmons with the new-and-improved Roni Kenway. In the two years she'd worked with Judd, he'd never indicated that he thought of her as anything other than one of the guys.

That was a compliment, in a way, because female mechanics weren't that thick on the ground in NASCAR, and she'd done her level best to fit in. But there was a huge difference between fitting in and becoming invisible. And it was time Judd's intense blue gaze registered on her when he looked her way. The man flipped all her switches. She knew when he approached by the scent of him—tangy after-shave that made her think of how he'd look in front of a bathroom mirror, a razor in one hand and nothing but a towel wrapped around his hips.

This demonstrated how far gone she was. She'd pictured him in the shower after the workday, water sluicing down his chest and over…well, everything.

She'd had endless debates with herself about the color and texture of his chest hair. She imagined it was the same chocolate brown as the hair on his head, and he'd have just enough to look manly, just enough to brush against a woman's bare skin when they… Confession time, she'd imagined making love with Judd Timmons.

Unfortunately, she had little hope he'd imagined making love to her. From his typical matter-of-fact expression when he looked at her, he apparently saw her as nothing more than a capable part of the Lovejoy racing team. She wanted him to see a hot babe, even if she was usually dressed like the guys in a brown-and-gold Nomex uniform with Goddess Chocolates emblazoned on the back.

When she'd discovered that the first race of the season at Daytona coincided with Valentine's Day, she'd taken that as a sign to get this party started. But here it was Friday morning, two days before race day, and she had yet to break out the makeup she'd bought over the Christmas holidays. After all her plans to dazzle him from Day One of preseason, she'd chickened out.

Instead of wearing her new clothes, one size smaller than her old stuff after two months on a diet, she'd appeared at the track in the comfortable jeans and faded NASCAR sweatshirts that hid her figure. Instead of styling her red hair the way she'd taught herself back in December after an expensive new cut, she'd pulled it into a ponytail as always. Her pricey makeup hadn't made an appearance until this morning, and now she'd messed it up because she was more nervous than a rookie waiting for that first green flag.

Grabbing the Visine out of her makeup bag, she held it over her stinging eye. Her cell phone played the opening bars of Coldplay's "Viva La Vida" at that critical moment, causing her to squirt a stream of liquid all over her face. She muttered a few more choice words.

A call from Lovejoy driver Tucker Merritt at this hour of the morning couldn't be good news. She was the closest thing he had to a friend on the Goddess Chocolates team, but she didn't think he'd call to chat this early. More likely he'd called because he had a problem.

She prayed that he hadn't suffered some misfortune that would keep him out of the race. That would suck on so many levels. Mopping her face with another tissue, she hurried into the bedroom. This day was not starting out well.

After taking a calming breath, she picked up the phone from the bedside table and answered it. "What's up, Tucker? You okay?"

"That son of a gun Timmons cancelled out of his part of the TV interview we were supposed to tape this morning."

Roni vaguely remembered the interview was on the schedule for midmorning. She had nothing to do with the media, so she hadn't paid much attention. "Is something wrong? Is he sick?"

"Hell, no, he's not sick. He just doesn't want to do the interview with me, so he's made up some garbage about how he has to concentrate on the car this morning so it'll be ready for this afternoon's practice."

Roni's stomach muscles tightened. All week she'd been hoping that the rift between Tucker and Judd would heal itself, but cancelling out of an interview wasn't a step in the right direction. Judd must still be ticked off about Loretta.

Last season Judd had dated a racing fan, a petite blonde named Loretta Sinclair. Seeing them together had been painful for Roni, but she'd endured, knowing Loretta was much more glamorous than Roni would ever be.

Then Judd and Loretta had broken up, but it was no cause for celebration. According to rumor, Tucker had seduced Loretta while she was still with Judd. With that story circulating, Loretta had wisely made herself scarce, but the relationship between Judd and Tucker was damaged, and team spirit had leaked out of the Goddess Chocolates crew like air from a punctured tire.

Roni had hoped the whole kerfuffle would be forgotten over Christmas break, but obviously it hadn't been. Tucker claimed to be innocent and Roni had given him the benefit of the doubt. She was in the minority, though. His playboy reputation worked against him as crew members aligned themselves with Judd.

She'd done her best not to take sides, because ultimately she wanted the two men to reconcile and get on with the business of racing. She wondered how she could diplomatically suggest that to Tucker. "Judd could be telling the truth about needing to concentrate on the car," she said. "I mean, it's the start of the season, and Daytona is—"

"You think I don't know that? It's even more reason to do the interview together. Everybody's talking about us not getting along, and if we show up on TV and act like we're friends, maybe the rumors will die down."

Tucker had a point, but Roni also knew that Judd hated making appearances under the best of circumstances. She made another stab at difusing Tucker's anger. "I wouldn't take this personally. You know Judd's not fond of the cameras. He's not glib like you."

"It's not rocket science! You sit in a chair, they ask

you questions, you answer the questions. Piece of cake."

"For you." Roni had seen the blond twenty-four-year-old work the media. He was a natural. "It's not a piece of cake for Judd."

"And I should care because…? He needs to do the interview anyway. Besides, this isn't stage fright. It's a slap in the face. He hates my guts."

"I have to believe you both can move past this. You're professionals and you used to be friends." When Roni had joined the team two years earlier, she'd been struck by the warmth between the crew chief and the driver. Judd had treated Tucker like a kid brother.

Tucker laughed bitterly. "He refuses to listen to anything I have to say. He's made up his mind about me, and so has most of the crew. You're one of the few people who hasn't assumed I'm guilty."

"Because you told me you're not."

"Yeah, I told Judd, too, but he—"

"Tucker, don't forget you have the full support of Jake Lovejoy. That's huge."

"I know." Tucker sighed. "If I didn't have Jake pulling for me, I'd wonder if this was all worth it, but because of him, I'll hang in there. Anyway, I don't have to take this BS from Timmons. I'm calling Lovejoy."

Roni sucked in a breath. "Don't do that. You'll only make things worse."

"Like it could get any worse."

It could, Roni knew. They had a whole season ahead of them in which things could get way worse. "Tucker, please. Let it go. Do the interview alone. You'll be amazing, as always."

"Nope. I'm calling Lovejoy. Timmons needs to be there."

She recognized that stubborn tone. Once Tucker dug in his heels, there was no changing his mind. "Okay. Good luck with the interview." She also prayed Tucker wouldn't get Judd in trouble. Starting the season on the owner's bad side wasn't a good idea.

"Thanks. So, are we on for pizza in your room tonight? If you'll put in the order, I'll bring the beer."

Friday night was the NASCAR Camping World Truck Series race, and last season Roni and Tucker had formed the habit of sharing a pizza and watching the race on TV in her hotel room. At first she'd thought it odd that he'd rather come to her hotel room than invite her to his private motor home parked at the track, but he said it relaxed him to get away from there for the evening.

She knew Tucker counted on the camaraderie, especially these days. Because of that she was tempted to use their pizza night as a bribe to keep him from calling Lovejoy.

But a plan was forming in her mind, and if Tucker chose to skip sharing a pizza with her the plan wouldn't work. "Sure, we can do that. Come over about six."

"See you then." Tucker hung up.

As Roni clicked off her phone, she began to plot. Somehow, some way, she'd maneuver Judd into stopping by her room tonight while Tucker was there. With her as referee, she might get these two blockheads to start talking to each other.

She had to admit that Judd might not appreciate her interference, and his resentment might screw up her romantic plans. But that would be true only if she failed. If she succeeded, it was a win-win situation.

As JUDD TIMMONS WALKED into the garage area on Friday morning, the scream of power tools blended with the roar of stock car engines being prepped for Sunday's race. He loved every decibel. His appreciative gaze swept the immaculate space where teams worked side by side, their efficient harmony in sharp contrast to the fierce competition that would take place this weekend.

Lovejoy fielded three teams in Sunday's race and tried not to show favoritism, but everyone on the circuit knew that he'd pinned his hopes on Tucker Merritt in the No. 414 car currently sponsored by Goddess Chocolates. Because of that sponsor, the No. 414 car's paint scheme was brown and gold with an eye-catching toga-clad woman painted on the hood.

Judd walked toward the car and inhaled his favorite perfume—the scent of burnt rubber mixed with exhaust fumes and hot motor oil. This was his dream job, or at least, it had been until Tucker had betrayed his trust.

Tucker was young, blond, charismatic and barely twenty-four. He was what Judd had yearned to be, what the football injury to his knee had prevented him from being—a NASCAR phenom. But Judd had accepted that disappointment and realized that his true calling had probably been crew chief, anyway.

He liked being the one who pulled it all together, the one in charge of the analytical side of the race. In large part due to Judd, Tucker had achieved some remarkable feats in his short career. Judd had taken satisfaction in that.

Or he had, until the ugly business with Loretta last year. He couldn't say for sure that the bad blood between him and Tucker had caused the season to go south toward the end, but he suspected it had been a big factor. He'd considered leaving the team, but that had seemed cowardly and likely to cause more rumors, so he'd stayed.

Now he wondered if that had been wise. Everything about the kid irritated him. How was Judd supposed to help Merritt take the No. 414 car to a winning season when all he wanted to do was cram Tucker's pearly whites down his throat?

Leaving now wasn't an option, though. No one with any sense of honor left a team at the beginning of the season. So he'd stick, which meant he had work to do. The No. 414 car hadn't performed well in the qualifying race, which meant Tucker would be starting Sunday's event at the back of the pack. Nobody on the team was happy about that.

As Judd headed over to join the rest of his crew already at work on the car, someone laid a hand on his shoulder. He turned and discovered Orville Fenster, the Lovejoy team manager. Orville motioned him outside and Judd blew out a breath. He had a pretty good idea what this was about.

Orville, a fiftysomething guy with a string-bean physique and not much hair, left the garage and strode across the tarmac toward the Lovejoy team hauler parked in the infield. It was understood that Judd would follow.

Besides transporting race cars, the gigantic hauler served as a combination clubhouse and meeting room, which made it the ideal place to discuss sensitive subjects. Orville probably wanted to talk about the TV interview Judd had cancelled out on.

Judd pulled the brim of his Goddess Chocolates ball cap lower over his eyes and stepped out into the sunshine. The forecast called for cold and clear—great for racing. The track sat empty with no practice sessions scheduled at the moment, but the infield buzzed with activity and several people called out to Orville and Judd as they made their way to the hauler.

Judd returned the greetings with a smile and a wave because he had no beef with any of those guys. Nope, only one person at the track made him see red. Too bad that one person drove the car Judd was in charge of.

Instead of going in through the open back of the hauler, Orville walked up the steps positioned at the side door, which confirmed Judd's suspicion that Orville intended to chew him out about the interview.

Judd removed his earplugs and tucked them in his pocket. "Why does this feel like you're taking me out behind the woodshed?"

Orville chuckled. "Not a bad analogy."

"Sorry to hear that." So it probably was about the interview. Orville outranked him, so if Orville insisted, Judd would have go through with it.

Orville opened the door and checked inside. "Good deal. Nobody's here."

"Which means you can work me over with a rubber hose and nobody will be the wiser."

"Dammit, Timmons, I don't like this situation any better than you do." Orville walked into the lounge area, furnished in neutral colors with comfy, stain-resistant furniture. Then he closed the door that led to the back of the hauler, ensuring their privacy. No one would come through that door without knocking first.

Moving to a laminated counter that contained a small sink and a coffeepot, Orville picked up the empty carafe. "I need coffee. Want some?"

"No, thanks." Judd ignored the two beige couches placed against the outside walls and remained standing. "Let's just get this over with so I can go back to the garage." Taking off his cap, he scrubbed his fingers through his hair.

Orville sighed and proceeded to make coffee. "You used to be a whole lot easier to get along with, Timmons."

Judd went still. Maybe he'd miscalculated the seriousness of the moment. "Do you want my resignation, Orville? Is that what this is about?"

"Hell, no." Orville punched the button on the coffeemaker and turned. "For one thing, that would be insane at the beginning of the season. For another thing, you're the best crew chief on the circuit, in my opinion. But Lovejoy isn't happy about this rift between you and Merritt. He thinks Merritt has the talent to become a real contender."

Judd snorted. He hadn't meant to, but it just came out. Okay, Merritt was a pretty good driver, and maybe he'd won quite a few races early in his career, thanks in large part to Judd's coaching.

"I take it you don't agree with Lovejoy." Orville gazed at Judd as if daring him to say something negative.

Judd tapped his hat against his thigh as he searched for the right words. "I, um, think he needs more seasoning."

"Oh, come off it, Timmons." Orville leaned

against the counter and folded his arms over his chest. "Merritt made a move on your girlfriend. Everybody knows what happened, and everybody thinks that sucks. But Merritt is Lovejoy's choice, so we have to put personal issues behind us and get some wins for the No. 414 car this season."

An angry flush crept up from Judd's collar. He wanted to ask if Merritt had been called on the carpet for his lack of loyalty in becoming involved with a teammate's girlfriend. But if Lovejoy had big plans for Merritt, then Judd might be expected to swallow that as the price of doing business.

Judd wasn't an unforgiving guy. He might be willing to overlook what had happened if Merritt had shown the slightest bit of remorse. Instead he still insisted he was innocent.

Fat chance of that. Judd had seen for himself how upset Loretta had been when she'd finally confessed, and he couldn't think of any reason she'd make up a story about cheating on him with Merritt. It wasn't as if she'd had anything to gain by doing that, and she had her reputation to think of.

But instead of showing remorse, Merritt had become increasingly antagonistic toward Judd. Merritt was the transgressor, so what the hell was his problem? Why was he giving Judd suspicious looks, as if he thought Judd would deliberately sabotage him? What a crock. Time to defend himself on that score.

"Look," he said to Orville. "I want the No. 414

car to win races, no matter what. If Tucker Merritt is Lovejoy's choice, then I'll do everything in my power to get him to Victory Lane."

"The fans don't believe that," Orville said. "And that's why you can't ditch the interview. Goddess Chocolates doesn't like the negative publicity this feud is generating and the company bigwigs are threatening to pull their sponsorship."

Judd massaged the back of his neck before glancing up at Orville in mute appeal. "But I hate being on TV."

"I know you do, son," Orville said, his voice softening.

"And TV hates me. I'm too blunt for TV. I don't know how to spin stuff. They'll be asking questions designed to showcase any bad feelings between Merritt and me. I could make everything worse by saying the wrong thing."

"You're selling yourself short. Just bring that famous Judd Timmons control to bear on the problem, and you'll do fine on TV. Besides, I'm afraid you have no choice in the matter. Merritt called Lovejoy after you cancelled this morning."

Judd swore under his breath.

"You know Merritt has Lovejoy's ear. We all know that. Anyway, Lovejoy contacted me and told me to make sure you showed up for the taping. In fact, I've been assigned to drive you over there."

"What, he doesn't think I can be trusted to go without a chaperone?"

Orville grinned. "He doesn't want to hear any creative excuses as to why you just couldn't seem to make it."

"Look, I need to be at the garage this morning. It's critical."

"You have a capable crew. Speaking of which, I've been meaning to talk to you about Roni Kenway. That young woman may be the best we've got when it comes to car setup."

Judd knew the subject was closed when Orville deliberately changed the topic. But this new subject was only marginally less volatile. Ever since hiring Roni he'd fought his attraction to her because his private code forbade a personal involvement with a crew member. So much could go wrong, and that could easily affect the smooth operation of the team.

He couldn't regret bringing her aboard, though, because she was terrific at her job. "Roni's great," he said. As always, he aimed for an enthusiastic yet impersonal tone.

"I was wondering what you'd think about promoting her to car chief."

"Hmm." Now there was a nightmare in the making. If he made her the car chief they'd work even more closely together, which would severely test his resolve. Yet if Orville liked the idea, Judd couldn't nix it and negatively impact Roni's career.

"I know you've been making do without a car chief ever since Butler left last season. I have to say Roni impresses me."

Judd nodded, buying time, trying to get his mind around the concept. "It would be a bold move, making her car chief."

"I think Roni could handle it, and the rest of the crew likes her. She's not a girly-girl, and she works like her hair's on fire."

Judd couldn't help smiling at that. "As red as it is, you probably couldn't tell if it was or not." He loved that bright mop of hair. He was also extremely grateful that Roni wasn't, as Orville had put it, a girly-girl. She was potent enough in her no-nonsense work clothes. If she ever wore something sexy, he'd be toast.

Through no fault of her own Roni had turned out to be somewhat of a complication for him. There was also her relationship with Merritt. She was far too friendly with the driver for Judd's taste. They were friendly in a nonsexual way, more of a brother-sister thing, but Judd still didn't like it.

"Roni's story is pretty interesting, too," Orville said.

"It is?" Judd hadn't allowed himself to think much about Roni's personal life before she showed up for a job interview with her girl-next-door freckles and sparkling green eyes. Instead he'd focused on her impressive record at training school and had convinced himself that's why he'd hired her on the spot.

But now that Orville had brought up her past, he wondered what Orville knew that he didn't. "What's special about her story?"

"You should ask her sometime." Orville poured his coffee into a Lovejoy Racing Team traveling mug. "But not now. Now you need to give your crew a heads-up that you'll be doing that interview at ten so they'll have to live without you for an hour or so."

CHAPTER TWO

RONI WALKED INTO THE garage, heart thumping like an engine in need of a valve job. After decking herself out in snug jeans and a sexy green sweater, after styling her hair with mousse so it would look like a man had been running eager fingers through it, after nearly blinding herself with a mascara wand, she wanted Judd to glance over at her and swallow his tongue.

That would be tough to do when he wasn't even there. Despite everyone on the Lovejoy team wearing the same uniform, Roni could always pick Judd out of the crowd. His shoulders were a little broader, his hips a little slimmer than anyone else on the crew. And he was taller, too—about two inches over six feet. At five-eight she'd never been considered short, but Judd made her feel dainty.

"Hey, Ron, what's with the hair and the outfit?" Derek Blevins, Lovejoy's engine specialist, walked over to her, carrying his ever-present tray of spark plugs. He was the only crew member who called her Ron, and although it was a nickname she didn't much like because it made her sound like a man, she'd never corrected him.

Early in her life she'd chosen Roni as a nice compromise—not as flowery as her full name of Veronica and not as masculine as the ultimate short form of Ron. But acceptance in the NASCAR world had always been more important to her than quibbling over her name.

She had to move closer to Derek and speak up in order to be heard over the noise in the garage. "I felt in the mood to dress up a little." She continued to scan the garage area for Judd.

"Nice."

She glanced at him. "Thanks." She appreciated the honest admiration in his eyes, but Derek wasn't the fish she'd hoped to catch. "Guess I'll get into my Nomex."

"In case you were wondering, Timmons is out in the hauler, talking to Fenster about something."

"Oh." Probably the interview. No doubt Fenster was informing Judd that he had to do it, after all.

"It's a shame he's not here to see how great you look," Derek said.

Roni's gaze snapped back to Derek's. Was she that obvious? From the sheepish expression on Derek's face, she concluded the answer was yes.

"I'll get my uniform." As she was leaving, she paused and turned back to him. "Does everybody know that I…have a bit of a crush?"

"Not everybody."

"Oh."

"Most everybody."

She felt like sinking beneath the polished concrete floor of the garage, but she found the courage to ask the ultimate question. "Does Judd know?"

"I don't think so. You know Judd. You have to hit him over the head, which is pretty much what Loretta did." Derek coughed. "Forget I said that. I don't want to talk about her."

"Me, either." Roni thought about her plan for tonight, which seemed incredibly naive and probably had no chance of working. Instead she'd probably ruin any likelihood that she'd ever get romantic with the crew chief. "Anyway, I'm glad Judd doesn't suspect that I...well, you know."

"But you'd better put on your uniform or he's liable to figure it out."

"Right." She hurried away. This was more complicated than she'd expected. She wanted Judd to notice her as a woman, but she'd prefer he didn't figure out that he was the sole motivation for her transformation.

And much as she hated to admit it, she had to give Loretta some credit. Thanks to Loretta's example, Roni had realized that she had to be less of a tomboy and more of a hot chick if she wanted to get Judd's attention.

Moments later she was clad in the brown-and-gold Nomex, but she still wore the makeup and she'd left her hair loose. That made her change in appearance more subtle, and maybe that was for the best.

She was crouched next to the car, checking the wear on the right rear tire when she heard one of the crew hail Judd by name, and the team shut down their power tools in anticipation of a word from the chief.

Her stupid pulse went crazy, as if she hadn't worked with him through two full racing seasons. She'd been part of these impromptu meetings dozens of times. It was no big deal.

Except it was a big deal today. She'd taken a step into unknown territory by making herself more attractive to capture his interest. She'd thought nobody would realize what she was up to, but apparently she'd been mistaken.

To underscore that situation, she was wearing makeup on the job, something she'd never done before. She'd also fixed her hair in a manner that was supposed to make a man think of sweaty sex according to the stylist in Jackson, Wyoming, where she'd had it cut while she was home over Christmas break.

The Goddess Chocolates ball cap she normally wore would ruin the look of her hair, so she'd taken a chance and left it off so Judd could see the new style.

Would Judd think of sweaty sex when he saw it? Would he even notice that anything was different?

Now that the moment was at hand, she wasn't sure if she wanted him to or not. Along with the rest of the crew, she stood and faced him, pulling off her goggles and letting them dangle around her neck.

Judd was frowning slightly as he waited for the last of the team members to put down their tools and join the small group. In a gesture that had become an endearing little habit Roni cherished, he took off his cap and stabbed his fingers through his short brown hair, making it more spiky than usual. Then he crammed the hat back on his head. He didn't look happy.

She should be plotting how she was going to get him to pay a visit to her hotel room tonight so she could initiate a peace talk between him and Tucker, but instead she wondered whether he'd noticed anything different about her. At one point she thought she'd detected a flicker in his blue eyes when he glanced at her, but maybe she'd imagined it.

"I have to tape a TV interview this morning." He made it sound like a trip to the dentist.

She hated that he was unhappy, but no matter what his mood, his deep baritone always sent shivers of pleasure down her spine. She needed to ignore that and dream up a reason for him to drop by tonight. *Think, Roni!*

"Sorry about that, chief," Derek said.

"Yeah, me, too. I'll be back as soon as possible."

She forced herself to concentrate on a plan instead

of getting lost in those blue eyes. Maybe she could indicate that she had some race-day strategy they needed to discuss in private. Something to do with the tires. She might be able to make that convincing. She could say that—

"I'm putting Roni in charge of testing while I'm gone."

"Me?" The word came out in a squeak of surprise.

His glance settled on her. "Is that a problem?"

She gulped. "Nope. Not a problem. I just wasn't expecting it." That was the understatement of the century.

"Okay, then." He moved in her direction. "If you have a minute, we need to talk about what I'd like you to have the team accomplish while I'm gone."

"Sure." *Act normal, idiot! He might not have noticed your hair and makeup, but he's putting you in charge.* How pathetic was it that she would rather he'd said something nice about her hair?

As the rest of the team went back to work, Judd outlined the suspension testing he wanted done while he was at the TV studio. She paid attention— she was too much of a pro not to—but she wasn't above multitasking. While the mechanic in her recorded the details of his shop talk, the woman in her watched those sculpted lips move and imagined what they'd feel like against hers.

How cool if his no-nonsense tone was a disguise for the lust he felt simply because he stood close to her and her sexy hairstyle. The beauty operator had promised the cut would make a man think of getting her naked. Roni mentally crossed her fingers and searched for some positive sign from Judd, like awareness in his eyes or a hitch in his breathing.

"I think that about covers it." His breathing was perfectly even. There wasn't a single spark of lust in his eyes, either.

Well, shoot. Any minute he would walk away, and although she hadn't made his pulse rate spike, she could still work on the other project. Now was the perfect time to throw out her suggestion to meet him later for a private discussion about…what was it again?

Oh, yeah. Tires. Tires and tire changes. Race-day strategy. She was passionate about that, but at the moment she'd rather just be passionate, period. She was ready to launch her campaign when he spoke again.

"Did you have a bad night?"

"No, why?"

"Well, your eyes look sort of red, and your hair…well, no offense, but it looks like you just crawled out of bed. If you forgot your hat, I can find you another one. That would help cover up your hair."

She gritted her teeth. Her attempt to look sexily disheveled had apparently come off as a massive hangover and a last-minute scramble to get to work. That's what she got for not practicing with the hair and the makeup. No wonder he wasn't drooling over her.

Too embarrassed to admit she'd put time into creating this sorry mess, she shrugged and tried for nonchalance. "I overslept. But don't worry about the hat. I'll live without it today."

"You're probably working too hard."

"Maybe." She was definitely working too hard at trying to attract his attention, and with zero results. Her idea of being a peacemaker was probably doomed, as well. She should stick to what she knew—the setup of a race car—and leave this relationship stuff to others.

"But I want you to know that all that hard work hasn't gone unnoticed," he said.

"I appreciate that." She'd appreciate even more some indication that he found her attractive, but that didn't seem likely. He admired her for her ability to adjust a car's suspension so it hugged the curves. Unfortunately he didn't seem the least bit interested in hugging her curves.

"Speaking of your work, I have something I'd like to talk to you about. I was thinking maybe tonight."

She stared at him. It was noisy in the garage, but she could swear he'd just given her the exact opening she needed to launch her peacemaking project. "Uh, sure. Tonight would be fine."

"Good. How about dinner? I could get us reservations somewhere." He made it sound like a business arrangement rather than a date.

That's because it was a business arrangement, she reminded herself. Whatever he had on his mind was most certainly connected to work. No personal component whatsoever. But she could still use this opportunity to mend fences. "Let's be spontaneous and decide later where we'll eat."

"Uh, okay." He seemed uneasy. "We can do that. When should I pick you up?"

She thought quickly. If Judd showed up first, she could stall until Tucker arrived. Then all she had to do was find a way to keep them both in the room long enough to air their differences.

If all went well, they could share the pizza and watch the truck competition together. She could ask Tucker to bring a six-pack of beer to go with the pizza. Then she had another thought. "When does your interview come on?"

"I think it's five-thirty."

"Perfect. Come by at five-thirty and we'll watch it together."

"Roni, I'd rather jab a sharp stick in my eye than watch myself on TV. I make it a point to stay out of viewing range."

"All right, but I want to watch it. How long will the interview take?"

"Probably about fifteen minutes."

"Then come by my hotel room about five-forty-five and we can take it from there."

"Sounds good. And don't worry. I won't keep

you out late. You look like you could use some sleep." He gave her a quick smile and left.

Well, that was a romantic parting shot. Not. Fortunately she didn't have a tire gauge in her hand, because she had the powerful urge to throw something at his retreating back.

And that made her a very ungrateful person. She'd spent years working to become good enough that a crew chief would want to reward her abilities, and now that seemed about to happen. When the team had lost its car chief at the end of last season, Roni had secretly yearned for the position. She had a hunch Judd might offer it to her tonight.

The car chief title would give her more responsibility and more glory. She'd be second-in-command to Judd, but if he was blind to everything but her talent with a wrench, working that closely with him would be torture.

The more she thought about becoming Judd's car chief, the more impossible it seemed, unless... She thought about what Derek had said. *You know Judd. You have to hit him over the head. That's what Loretta did.*

Derek was right. Roni hadn't hit Judd over the head. She'd barely tapped him on the shoulder. If she intended to seduce Judd Timmons—and she might as well admit that was her goal—then she couldn't be halfhearted about it. She had to give it everything she had.

JUDD WAS SO DISTRACTED by Roni and her do-me-now hair that he didn't think about whether Merritt would be in the car until he climbed into the passenger seat of Orville's rented Toyota and discovered the backseat was empty. Orville said that Merritt had other appearances scheduled and would meet them over there. Judd was willing to take whatever breaks came his way.

"Saves you having to make small talk," Orville said as they drove away from the speedway.

After being blindsided by Roni's new look, Judd wouldn't have been capable of that, anyway. He was not in control of his situation with Roni or with Tucker, and he hated that feeling. "You know, I need to deal with Tucker or think about switching to another team at the end of the season."

"I'm asking you not to think like that, Judd. The kid's young. He may or may not stick around."

"In other words, I should find a way to tolerate Merritt. You know, over Christmas break I convinced myself I could do that. But his paranoia is hard to take. He questions everything I say to him, as if he thinks I'm trying to sabotage his career."

"I've noticed that." Orville drove with the practiced ease of a former race car driver. "Want me to have a talk with him?"

Judd wasn't crazy about that option. He should be able to handle his own problems. "Let's see what happens this weekend."

"I just don't want him to run you off. I doubt the rest of the crew would be happy about that, either."

"*I* wouldn't be happy about that. It's an outstanding bunch of guys."

"And one woman."

"Right." He wondered if he'd used the word *guys* on purpose. Probably. But his attempt to make Roni one of the guys was failing miserably. "You know what I meant."

Orville smiled.

"What's so funny?"

"You. You work so hard to prove to everyone that you don't notice Roni is a woman, which tells me you notice all the time."

"I think of her as a talented mechanic. That's it." Sure he did. For the umpteenth time, he pictured the way she'd looked this morning with her hair mussed up, as if she'd just had sex with some guy.

He knew she hadn't. If Roni was seeing someone, he'd be aware of it. Not that he kept track of her dating life...well, maybe he did. That was only natural. She was part of his crew.

And you don't want to see her hook up with somebody because you want her yourself, whispered the voice of his conscience. This morning he'd managed to have a normal conversation with her about the testing he wanted done, but the whole time he'd been having visions of Roni naked.

"Okay," Orville said. "I could be wrong that you're

interested in her. I've been known to be wrong before."

"I'm interested in her abilities as a mechanic," Judd said. "I have an appointment with her for late this afternoon, and I plan to take your suggestion and offer her the car chief job." He decided not to mention they were going to dinner. Orville would probably make something of that, and it wasn't anything more than a chance to offer her the job in a quiet setting, but at the same time a public setting.

Orville nodded. "Good. See, I can tell you don't want to leave this team right when it's coming together so nicely."

"I don't want to leave this team at all, which is why I'm going into that studio prepared to be Tucker Merritt's new best friend. I want Jake Lovejoy to watch this show tonight and beam with pleasure."

Orville parked the car in the studio lot and glanced at Judd. "Don't overdo it, Timmons."

"With a guy as out there as Merritt, I don't even think that's possible." As Judd walked into the studio, he thought about Roni watching the show later tonight. Sad to say, he cared more about her reaction than Lovejoy's.

CHAPTER THREE

PRACTICE THAT AFTERNOON wasn't what Roni would call a barrel of laughs. She got so sick of listening to Judd and Tucker squabble, she was tempted to rip off her headset and take a cigarette break even though she didn't smoke.

"The car's too loose, Timmons," Tucker complained after a couple of laps. There was a definite edge to his voice, as if he might be accusing Judd of making it that way on purpose.

Judd's reply crackled through Roni's headset. "Yesterday you said it was too tight."

"Then somebody overcompensated," Tucker said. "I'm fishtailing all over the place."

"Bring it in and we'll take a look." Judd seemed to be making a supreme effort not to lose his temper.

Roni appreciated that effort. Somebody needed to be the grownup, and Tucker wasn't a good candidate. Apparently the interview had not gone well for Tucker. Roni was dying to see it and find out what was sticking in Tucker's craw.

Tucker brought the car onto pit road, and Roni

worked her magic, adding wedge to the springs and applying everything she'd learned about tire stagger during her training.

Tucker went back on the track, but he still wasn't pleased with the handling.

"Look, Merritt," Judd said at one point, "we're doing the best we can."

"I'm sure Roni is," Tucker shot back, and his implication was clear. Roni was trying to help and Judd was trying to hinder.

She didn't have a mike, so she couldn't talk to Tucker, but she would have liked to give him a piece of her mind. How could he imagine that Judd wanted him to fail on Sunday? If Tucker failed, the whole team failed, including Judd. Judd might be bullheaded, but he wasn't about to commit career suicide by sabotaging Tucker's car.

Ordinarily she loved her job, but she was glad to leave the track at quitting time and rush back to the hotel to shower and change before her two bad boys showed up.

After phoning in the pizza order, she jumped into the shower. Her cleanup routine had to be quick, and she'd decided in advance that she'd wear a low-cut turquoise silk blouse that made her eyes look almost blue, and snug black jeans that showed off her figure. Her boots had a three-inch heel, and she added large gold hoop earrings because she'd noticed that Loretta favored those.

After Judd's comment about her hair, she didn't feel comfortable leaving it down, so she swept it up on top of her head and fastened it with a few hairpins. With luck, it would stay put. With even more luck, Judd would remove the pins later on tonight.

Because of time constraints, she'd have to apply her makeup while she watched the interview, but she wasn't about to miss it. Seeing the two men together on camera would give her a clue as to how to approach the evening ahead.

She grabbed the remote, sat on the end of her bed with her makeup at her side, and turned on the TV. She was familiar with this show, and the set was the same as always—gray swivel chairs grouped around an oak coffee table. Kurt Donovan, a man who looked like a graying version of Elvis, conducted the interviews.

The show started with a close-up of Kurt, who obviously loved NASCAR with a passion. He talked about the historical significance of Daytona and ran a brief retrospective of those who had won it.

"But this race is never predictable," Kurt said, "and we have a dark horse in the studio, along with his crew chief. There's been some controversy surrounding this duo recently, but if they can put it together on Sunday, they have the talent to take home all the marbles. Please welcome from the Lovejoy team Tucker Merritt and his crew chief, Judd Timmons."

Roni stared at the screen, her makeup forgotten

as the camera angle widened to reveal Judd on Kurt's left, looking incredibly yummy in khaki slacks and a white polo with the Lovejoy Racing emblem on the breast pocket. No doubt about it, Judd was gorgeous. He might hate cameras, but they loved him.

He wore the obligatory brown-and-gold Goddess Chocolates promo cap. Such a shame to cover up that thick brown hair, but the sponsor would expect him to wear the hat. Judd turned to look at Kurt, and his sculpted jaw and strong nose made for a compelling profile.

She remembered that he and his compelling profile would be knocking on her door in about fifteen minutes and she picked up her mirrored compact containing her pressed powder.

Tucker was on screen, too, of course, but she didn't take much notice. By chance or design, both men were dressed alike, with identical Goddess Chocolates caps. Women swooned over Tucker's blond good looks, but Roni thought he was too much of a pretty boy. She preferred a face like Judd's, more chiseled, more indicative of his strength of character.

Her judgment might be clouded by the practice this afternoon, but Tucker looked really young to her, and he fidgeted in his chair. Judd sat quietly. He might be going crazy with nerves, but it didn't show. Roni admired the courage he demonstrated by sitting there as if he did this kind of interview every day for fun.

"So." Kurt swiveled his chair to look at each of

his guests in turn. "I hope I won't be taking my life in my hands, sitting between you two. Rumor has it there's trouble in the Lovejoy camp. I'd hate to end up in the middle of a brawl."

"That's not a possibility." Judd looked completely at ease. "I believe in keeping everything civilized, don't you, Tucker?"

Roni was fascinated. From somewhere deep inside, Judd had found the ability to weather this television appearance. His calm delivery was completely convincing.

"To a degree," Tucker said. "But in the long run, it's survival of the fittest."

"In that case," Judd said, with a smile that moved through Roni's system like warm syrup, "you should do fine, Tucker. You have talent to burn."

"Yeah, but I—" Tucker's sudden realization that Judd had paid him a compliment was funny to watch. He turned slowly toward the crew chief, his eyes wide with shock. His mouth opened and closed again. Finally he mumbled "Thanks," and seemed to sink into his chair.

Roni was fascinated. She'd never seen Tucker thrown off his game. He'd obviously been ready to spar with Judd, and Judd hadn't obliged him. She could only imagine what giving Tucker that praise had cost him, but he'd risen to the occasion. Tucker's scowl told her why the afternoon's practice hadn't gone well. Tucker had been upstaged, and he'd hated that.

Kurt seemed to sense the shift in power and focused on Judd. "I'm sure each crew chief has a certain style. How would you define yours?"

"Intense concentration, but always staying flexible. You have to be when anything could happen out there."

Roni beamed. Excellent answer.

"That's for sure." Tucker leaned forward, as if trying to dredge up his usual charisma and recapture the spotlight. "There was this one time, when the No. 53 car was about to run up on me, and I tried to block him, but then in front of me, the No. 76 car spun out, and I was all *oh, man, what now?*"

Kurt allowed Tucker to carry on awhile longer about his various close calls, and maybe there were fans out there who loved to hear that, but Roni thought Tucker came across like a little kid shouting *Look at me!*

Eventually Kurt had to interrupt for a commercial break, and Roni frantically applied her makeup during that sixty seconds. It was no masterpiece, but it would have to do. Judd hadn't noticed her makeup this morning, so she wasn't too worried. She thought he'd notice her blue silk blouse and bun-hugging jeans, though.

When Kurt came back on camera, he turned his attention immediately to Judd, as if he didn't want to give Tucker a chance to get wound up again. "The crew chief is essential to a win on Sunday. What's your strategy?"

"We have a top-notch crew," Judd said, "and Tucker's an outstanding driver, although I know even he'd admit that he has a lot to learn about racing."

Roni winced. Okay, so Judd wasn't willing to be completely gracious.

Tucker puffed out his chest. "Some things are instinctive," he said. "They can't be taught."

"I agree." Judd gazed at him. "And if you combine good instincts with being coachable, you have something special."

"So what's your evaluation, Judd?" Kurt looked extremely pleased that his two guests were exhibiting some antagonism toward each other, after all. "Is Tucker Merritt coachable?"

Judd faltered for the first time in the interview. "He can be," he said at last.

"Can be?" Kurt prompted.

"What are you getting at, Timmons?" Tucker half rose from his chair.

Judd seemed to give himself a mental shake. "Nothing. We're going to be an outstanding team on Sunday."

"Worth watching, for sure." Kurt continued to focus on Judd. "Every crew chief has a nickname. What's yours?"

Judd started to answer, but Tucker beat him to it. "He's the Iceman," Tucker said. "Trust me, he's earned that name, too." If Tucker had been smiling, the comment could be taken as praise. But he hadn't been smiling.

Roni wondered what Lovejoy would think of the interview. But she didn't have time to worry about that right now. The Iceman was at her door.

JUDD FELT LIKE A KID on a first date. But this wasn't a date, he told himself sternly. Sure, he'd showered and changed into slacks and a long-sleeved dress shirt. He'd left his Goddess Chocolates cap back in his hotel room, but he'd worn his Lovejoy team jacket complete with sponsor patches. It wasn't like he'd opted for a sport coat.

But he'd thought about it.

Roni opened the door, and he forgot to breathe. No fair. She wasn't supposed to dress like this, dammit! Those big gold hoops wouldn't be appropriate in the garage, and that red hair piled on top of her head was far too sexy for a mechanic. No ball cap for her, either.

His gaze moved lower. Until this moment, he'd been able to push all thoughts of Roni's curves to the far recesses of his brain. He could scarcely ignore the subject now.

They were showcased in a blouse that had the sheen of silk and was a vibrant turquoise blue. The material dipped in exactly the right place. Lord help him. He was in big trouble.

His problems didn't end with the blouse, either. She'd tucked it into a pair of black jeans that should require a license to wear them in public. From the way they fit in front, he could imagine how they fit in back, and a sight like that could move a grown man to tears—either from joy or frustration, depending upon his likelihood of gaining access to what was inside those jeans.

Last of all, Judd noticed the boots. The pointed toe and sassy heel were like nothing he'd ever seen on Roni's feet before. Good thing, too, because if he intended to keep his sanity, he should advise her never to wear those boots again. A guy could exercise only so much restraint before he snapped.

The real killer in this scenario was Roni's warm smile, which made him ache to grab her and kiss her until they were both breathless. But he would not. He *would not*.

"The interview was very good," she said.

A long two seconds went by before he remembered what interview she was talking about. The present was too engrossing for him to drag himself into the past. When confronted with Roni in blue silk and black denim, Judd could barely remember his name, let alone what had happened this morning.

But a response was called for. It took him forever to recall the usual reply to such a compliment. Finally he came up with it. "Thanks."

"Come on in a minute, okay? I'm not quite ready."

Ready for what? His fevered brain wondered what else she could do to make herself desirable. The cautious side of him didn't want to know, and the wild side, the side that had longed to be a NASCAR champion, couldn't wait. He didn't welcome the return of that reckless kid he used to be.

"Make yourself comfortable." She gestured toward the two chairs sitting on either side of a small table over by the window. The curtains were closed. "I'll only be a second."

He walked into the room as instructed, but in his current frame of mind, being alone with Roni in a room with a bed was a really bad idea. They wouldn't be staying here, though. They needed to be driving somewhere. Anywhere.

Previously he'd thought the dining room in this hotel would work, but now he could see it was entirely too close to Roni's room on the second floor. A bottle of wine, a few laughs, some heated glances, and he'd be suggesting they continue the discussion upstairs. He'd come here to ask her to be his car chief, not his lover.

Fortunately, he was staying in a totally different hotel, and he needed to make sure that was always the case for the rest of the season now that he realized that Roni wasn't quite the tomboy he'd imagined her to be. As the old saying went, she cleaned up real good. Too good.

She scooped up some things from the end of the bed and walked into the bathroom, but she left the door open. The scene was way too cozy. Her stuff was scattered around, although not in a messy way.

The room looked lived-in, similar to the way he inhabited a hotel room.

A book on the history of auto racing, one he'd been meaning to pick up, lay on her nightstand, along with a framed picture of Roni with some guys who looked like cowboys. He thought of Orville's comment that she had an interesting background and decided to ask her about it during dinner.

"I can see why Tucker was upset after the interview, though," she called from the bathroom. "He didn't get to be his usual charming self."

"The whole thing was a weird experience. I was determined to make it go well, but when Donovan asked me the coachability question, I couldn't lie. Tucker's anything but coachable these days." The room was warm, so he took off his jacket and laid it on one of the chairs.

"You did a good job. You seemed a lot more at ease."

"Thanks." He'd already said that once, but he couldn't come up with a better comment, especially while he was being bombarded with all things Roni. The room smelled like her, although until now he'd never identified a particular scent as hers. He identified it now—lemony and fresh, but with an undertone of something more erotic.

In the past he'd laughed at the theory of pheromones, but he was beginning to think they existed, after all. In the garage, her intriguing scent had been overridden by exhaust fumes, but in this room he got a full blast of it. His body reacted, and if they didn't head for a restaurant soon, he couldn't guarantee they'd make it there at all. He was having very inappropriate thoughts about Roni and that king-size bed that took up most of the hotel room.

She walked out of the bathroom, and he couldn't tell that she'd done anything more to herself than putting on a delicate gold chain that nestled against her skin and drew his attention to the curves he was trying so hard to ignore. He had the crazy thought that she was stalling, but he couldn't imagine why.

"I have an idea." She stood on the far side of the room. "What would you think of ordering a pizza and staying here?"

Professionally, it was a dangerous plan. Personally, he loved it. "We should probably go out." He wondered if she'd understand why he'd said that.

"Judd, I have a confession to make. I brought you here for a specific reason."

His jaw dropped. Was she really about to proposition him? His pulse leaped at the idea. But he couldn't let that happen. That would be such a mistake. It would be so...wonderful.

Her cheeks flushed, making her freckles stand out. "I can tell what you're thinking, and...wow, this is complicated. But let's start with Tucker. He's the main reason I asked you to come to my room tonight, and why I suggested staying here to share a pizza."

"Tucker?" That name was exactly what he needed to hear in order to cool his overheated engine.

Her cheeks grew even redder. "Tucker's due here in a couple of minutes."

He stared at her. Now that she'd mentioned Tucker, he remembered that she and Tucker usually spent Friday nights together, watching the truck race. He'd assumed when she agreed to have dinner with him that she wasn't seeing Tucker tonight. "What's going on, Roni?"

She looked painfully uncomfortable with the situation, but to her credit, she took a deep breath and plunged on. "I thought that maybe, if the two of you had a quiet place to talk, to work through your differences, that…that…"

Watching her take that deep breath had revved his engine again, but all he had to do was think of Tucker arriving any minute, and he calmed right down. "You were setting yourself up as an arbitrator?"

She groaned. "It seemed like a good idea at the time. Nobody else is doing anything, and so I—"

"You were going to referee dressed like *that?*"

She glanced down at her outfit and back up at him. "I wanted you—well, both of you, I guess—to realize I'm not a kid."

"Mission accomplished." His heart twisted. He'd thought she'd chosen her clothes to impress him, but she'd probably done it for Tucker. Women did like to impress that guy. "Roni, it's a goodhearted impulse, but maybe I should just leave and let you spend the evening with Tucker." And chalk up another victory for the golden boy.

"Don't go. Let's just try this. You're both away from the track, away from the cameras and the microphones. Have you had any chance to simply talk about the problem?"

"Well, no, but—"

"The team is in trouble, Judd."

He scrubbed his hands through his hair. "I know."

"What have you got to lose?"

When she put it that way, and he understood how earnestly she'd planned this meeting, he couldn't just walk out. Maybe she was right. Maybe he and Tucker could talk in this room and find some way to repair the damage to their relationship.

"Okay. I'll stay."

Her shoulders relaxed and she smiled. "Great. Thanks. Like I said, he should be here any—" A tap on the door made her turn in that direction. "There he is."

Judd stood with his hands in his pockets as Roni opened the door. Over her shoulder he could see Tucker's wide smile fade as he glimpsed Judd standing behind her.

"What the hell's he doing here?" He held up a six-pack of beer. "I thought we were having pizza together."

"We are. I asked Judd to come by because I

thought the privacy of my hotel room would be a good place for the two of you to talk."

Tucker's jaw worked as he glared at Judd. "Got nothing to say to him. I can't believe you did this, Roni."

Judd stepped forward. "She's only trying to help, Merritt. Our problems are affecting the team, and this would be a safe place to air our differences. No media. No other team members except Roni. I'm sure we can trust her not to discuss what's said here."

Tucker's facial muscles tightened. "It's a moot point, because nothing's going to be said here." He shoved the beer at Roni and the cans clunked together. "You two might as well enjoy this."

Roni grabbed the beer, barely saving it from dropping to the floor. "Wait, Tucker. I should have told you about this, but I thought—"

"You thought wrong. See you both at the track." Tucker headed back down the hall.

"I wish you'd reconsider," Roni called after him.

There was no reply.

She turned back to Judd, a self-mocking smile on her kissable lips. "That certainly went well." The smile didn't hide the misery in her green eyes. "I'm sorry, Judd. Instead of making things better, I've made them worse."

Judd's heart went out to her. She'd meant to do a good thing, and because Tucker was a jerk, it had blown up in her face. She'd been brave enough to try something when no one else seemed to know how to approach the issue.

She was still being brave, determined that he wouldn't see her embarrassment at having failed so spectacularly. He should probably leave, too, but he couldn't do that and leave her to wallow in the aftermath of this disaster.

Staying was dangerous, though. His private code of conduct, the one that warned him against becoming personally involved with Roni, was in serious jeopardy. But she looked so miserable, and he wanted to comfort her somehow.

He reached for the beer. "Let me take that."

"Oh." She seemed to have forgotten she was holding the six-pack. "I don't suppose you'd like to—"

"Stay for pizza? Sure." He was on a slippery slope, but he'd stay for pizza. Over pizza, he'd offer her the car chief job, which should cheer her up. Then he'd leave with his code intact.

Her shoulders sagged in obvious relief. "You're not upset with me?"

"Why would I be?" He fought the impulse to touch her, to reassure her that everything was okay.

"Because I meddled in something that was none of my business. I overstepped, and the last thing in the world I want is for you to be upset."

As he gazed into her green eyes, he forgot why his code was so damned important. Setting the beer on the floor, he drew her into his arms. "I'm not upset."

CHAPTER FOUR

RONI COULDN'T HAVE predicted this move of Judd's in a million years. She was in a state of shock as he lowered his mouth to hers.

She had no idea if this miracle would ever happen again. Maybe it wasn't even happening at all. She'd dreamed of Judd's kiss dozens of times, and this could be another one of her nighttime fantasies.

But whether his kiss was real or not, she vowed to milk every last ounce of pleasure from it. The first velvet contact made her dizzy enough to clutch his shoulders for support. Those shoulders felt solid and muscular under the cotton of his dress shirt, so maybe she wasn't dreaming, after all.

He tasted delicious, a combination of mint and coffee. His lips moved gently, finding the perfect fit. And there it was. Perfection. A thrill of recognition shot through her as he settled in with a soft sigh. This was so *right*.

The kiss began slowly, almost lazily. Deceptive, that slow pace. He turned the heat up so gradually that she missed the transition from sweet and warm to panting and hot. Somehow they'd made that transition, though, because his tongue was very busy and his fingers were buried in her hair. Pins scattered to the carpet as he cradled her head and deepened the kiss.

He lifted his mouth a fraction from hers, and he was breathing hard. "Roni, you're killing me."

"Then maybe you should lie down until you feel better."

With a groan, he captured her mouth again and her heart raced out of control. She had Judd alone in her hotel room. The bed was only a few feet away.

At the second when she thought he'd crack and edge her toward the mattress, he released her and backed away. Gasping, he shook his head. "Sorry."

She dragged in a breath. "I'm not."

"I'm not sure I am, either, but I should be." He gazed at her, his blue eyes still glazed with passion. "Kissing you was not part of my plan, let alone..." He gestured toward the bed.

"What was your plan?"

"To have dinner and offer you the car chief job." He shoved his fingers through his hair. "I never intended for us to become so...involved."

"Because you don't want me sleeping my way to the top?" She smiled at him. He was adorably ethical, and she thought that was a fine thing indeed. But it had its place, and now was not the time to be noble.

He didn't return her smile. "Obviously, I'm attracted to you, but—"

"Well, thank God for that. I've had a crush on you forever."

"You've had a crush on me? How did I miss that?"

"As Derek pointed out today, you tend not to notice such things. He said a woman has to hit you over the head." She swept a hand down her outfit. "This is my version of bashing you with a two-by-four."

"So you didn't get dressed up for Tucker?" He seemed surprised.

"Of course not. Tucker's like a brother to me."

"You parade around like that a few more times and you might discover he's not feeling so brotherly."

Some of the warmth went out of the room. Roni didn't have to be a genius to figure it out. Tucker had moved in on the last woman Judd had been involved with. Judd didn't know Roni well enough to trust her not to do the same.

Another knock sounded at the door.

Judd looked at Roni. "It could be him, rethinking his position."

Instinctively her hands went to her hair, which was a dead giveaway that something major had happened between her and Judd.

"You'd better go into the bathroom and fix it," Judd said. "I'd rather he didn't know what just happened."

"Would you rather nobody knows?" A little more of her happiness slipped away.

"It's none of anybody's business, is it?"

She sighed. "Guess not." She could understand that he'd be worried about gossip, but she didn't think they'd done anything to be ashamed of.

"Do I have any lipstick on me?" he asked.

She shook her head. "This is pricey stuff. It won't come off on you. You get the door, and I'll go fix my hair." She walked into the bathroom and closed the door.

She could hear Judd talking to someone, and shortly after that he knocked on the bathroom door.

"It wasn't Tucker," he said. "It was the pizza delivery guy."

She should have been disappointed that Tucker hadn't returned to the bargaining table. Instead she was selfishly happy that she and Judd were still alone. She jabbed the last pin in place and opened the door. "I honestly forgot I'd ordered it."

"By some coincidence you got my favorite— mushroom, sausage and tomato."

"What do you know?" Maybe later she'd tell him that it was no coincidence. After two years of paying attention to his likes and dislikes, she knew what his favorite pizza was. But at the moment she didn't feel like revealing that much. If he wanted to keep their hot kiss secret, she wasn't sure exactly where she stood.

He wanted her, no doubt about that. But he didn't seem happy about wanting her. Until she fully understood his thinking, she'd play her cards close to her vest.

"So we have pizza and beer," she said. "What more do we need?"

"I'd planned on taking you out to dinner."

"Assuming you paid for that pizza, you just bought me dinner. It seems silly to let it go to waste. And we could watch the truck race while we eat."

"I'm sure somebody will TiVo it. I think we need to talk."

"That sounds ominous."

He grimaced. "I didn't mean it to. I just—"

"Look, if you want to pretend that kiss never happened, we'll do that." It would break her heart, but she hated seeing him so uncomfortable.

He glanced at her. "Not much chance I'll forget it, Roni."

"Actually, me, either." She wanted to do it again. Judging by the heat in his gaze, so did he.

"We need to change the subject." Breaking eye contact, he walked over to the table by the window where he'd set the pizza box and the six-pack. "Can I open a beer for you?"

"Sure. Thanks."

Judd popped the top on a beer and handed it to her. She felt a moment of guilt for drinking the beer that Tucker had brought because he thought they'd be hanging out together. Instead, he was probably sitting alone in his motor home.

"I feel sort of bad about misleading Tucker." She sat down in one of the two chairs flanking the table.

"But not about misleading me?" Judd took the other chair and flipped open the pizza box. The aroma of melted cheese and cooked sausage wafted upward.

"I feel bad about that, too. I should have just told each of you what I hoped to accomplish and then let you decide if you wanted to be a part of it."

Judd handed her a napkin. "We both would have refused. I can almost guarantee it. An ambush was the only way, and it almost worked." He gestured toward the pizza. "Dig in."

"I'm not ready to give up on this problem." Roni surveyed the pizza and chose one of the smaller slices. "If you two don't bury the hatchet, this will dog us throughout the season."

"All I need is an apology." Judd picked up a wedge of pizza. "Instead, he acts as if I'm the one who's done something wrong. I'll meet him halfway, but groveling isn't my style."

"I wouldn't ask you to do that. But what if I convinced him to meet here tomorrow night? What if I told him that you want to talk things out for the good of the team? I know, deep down, he admires you. He's an only child, and you're like a big brother to him."

Judd swallowed a bite of pizza. "Then he should have stayed away from my girlfriend, shouldn't he?"

She hesitated, not sure of her ground. "Have you ever considered that he's telling the truth, that he didn't do it?"

"I don't know why Loretta would lie about a thing like that."

Roni had no answer. She wanted to believe Tucker was innocent, but he might not be. "Haven't you ever made a mistake you'd chalk up to immaturity?"

Judd paused in the act of picking up another slice of pizza. Then he gave her a sheepish grin. "You mean like playing football on an injured knee because I wanted the glory of being the quarterback who won the Big Ten championship for Indiana?"

"That would qualify, but I can beat that for sheer stupidity."

"Let's hear it. Orville said you had an interesting story. I never asked anything about your life before you graduated from your NASCAR training. I think…I think I was afraid the more I knew, the more I'd be attracted to you."

"And what's so awful about that?" She thought of all the times she'd wished he would notice her, and he'd been deliberately avoiding that.

"I've only been a crew chief for six years, and you're the first woman I've ever hired. I didn't want to think hiring you had anything to do with me finding you sexy."

"Did it?" She took a gulp of beer, not sure which way she wanted him to answer.

"No." He blew out a breath. "I was very impressed with your training record. I would have hired you if you'd been a Martian with one eye in the middle of your forehead."

That made her laugh.

"But it didn't hurt that you were a cute redhead with a terrific body." He finished off his beer and set the can aside. "So now you have all you need to have me locked up for sexual harassment."

"Are you seriously worried about that? Because I would never—"

"I know you wouldn't," he said quietly. "It's not fear of a lawsuit that's freaking me out. It's the potential for a team catastrophe. We already have this issue between Tucker and me gumming up the works. As you well know, personal problems can wreck a team."

"There's no guarantee you and I would end up with a problem."

He met her gaze. "There's no guarantee we wouldn't, either. As the crew chief, it's my job to minimize the possibility of disaster."

"But you're attracted to me."

"Obviously, but—"

"Do you want me to quit?"

He looked horrified. "God, no. You're a huge asset. Orville would have my hide if you quit. No, I'm going to handle this attraction. I'm going to deal with it."

"Okay." Thinking back to that scorching kiss, she wondered if he'd succeed. "Is there anything I can do to help?"

"Not really. This is my problem and I'll just... handle it."

"Okay."

"Which means I should take off pretty soon, but first I really have to ask, what's the big mistake in your past that makes you so eager to defend Merritt?"

"I was a juvenile delinquent."

"No, you weren't." He shook his head and set aside his empty beer can. "I don't believe that for a minute."

"Ask anybody at the Last Chance Ranch."

"The whozit?"

"It's a place in Jackson Hole, Wyoming. These days they raise cutting horses, but it's more than a business operation. It's..." Roni was hit with a sudden wave of homesickness. "It's the most beautiful place on earth."

"Go on."

She found herself talking about things she seldom mentioned to anyone—how she'd run away at sixteen to escape a stepfather who beat her, and how she'd been picked up while hitchhiking by a ranch hand from Last Chance.

"The Chance family gave me a hot meal, a place to shower, and a warm bunk," she said. "I repaid them by hot-wiring one of the ranch trucks so I could steal it."

"I find that so hard to believe."

"I was out for *numero uno*." Roni marveled that she hadn't ended up a criminal. "They caught me before I got far and made me a deal. If I'd keep the ranch trucks running, they wouldn't press charges. I was looking at being locked up in some juvenile detention facility, so of course I agreed. Then I proceeded to soup up the ranch trucks and talk the younger hands into drag racing with me."

"I'll take a wild guess those are the guys in the picture."

"Yep. We had some fun times stirring up dust on the ranch roads. Then I heard about NASCAR and saved my money so I could afford to train at the institute. After that I looked for a job."

"Did you apply with all the racing teams?"

She shook her head.

"How many?"

"Just Lovejoy."

"Really?" He leaned forward, clearly amazed. "Why only us?"

"I don't think I should tell you."

"Come on, Roni. You can't tell everything else and leave out this part."

She drank the last of her beer. "All right. I saw you on TV."

"I'm hardly ever on TV."

"I know, but I happened to catch a show where you were one of the guests."

"Was I terrible?"

"Yep."

He winced. "At least you're honest, but I don't understand how watching me give a terrible interview would make you want to work with Lovejoy Racing."

"You were so bad that you made me smile, and there was something about you, about your approach to racing…" She gave up all pretence. "I was hot for you, okay? Happy now?"

Judd leaned back in his chair and stared at her. "Does Orville know this part of the story?"

"No."

"What did you tell Orville?"

"I made my decision seem mystical. See, there's a spot on the ranch that's sacred to the Shoshone Indians. I ride out there when I have a tough decision to make."

"We're talking on horseback, right?"

"Well, duh. It's a *ranch*. Anyway, at that special place I always find clarity. I told Orville that it was after a visit there that I decided to apply at Lovejoy Racing."

Judd studied her. "Hmm."

"It's partly true. I did ride out there and ask if I should apply for a job with the outfit that had the hot young crew chief."

"And the answer?"

"The answer that came to me was a definite yes."

Judd blew out a breath. "To think I snapped you up that day because I thought you'd have applications in everywhere and I didn't want another team to get you." He paused to gaze at her. "What would you have done if I hadn't hired you?"

"Gone back out to the Shoshone sacred spot, I guess, and asked what the eff was going on."

"You may still have to make a trip back out there, Roni, because I'm gonna do my damnedest to keep my hands to myself from now on."

"That's a shame."

"I know." He shoved back his chair and picked up his jacket. "But it's for the best."

CHAPTER FIVE

JUDD DIDN'T EXPECT to get much sleep once he returned to his hotel room, but to his surprise he dozed off immediately. After some sizzling dreams about Roni, he woke up in a better mood than he'd enjoyed in a long time. Apparently he'd needed the ego boost of knowing Roni thought he was hot. His challenge would lie in knowing how she felt and not doing anything about it.

When he walked into the noisy garage, she was already there. He caught sight of her right before she disappeared under the car, and he noticed that her hair was back in its ponytail and she was wearing her hat. No sexy style today, no revealing blue silk, no tight black denim.

He wondered if she'd tried to do him a favor so he wouldn't be tempted. If so, it wasn't working. Roni had his full attention even when she showed up in her uniform with her ponytail sticking out the backside of her sponsor cap.

Concentrating on his work today would be tough. Or not. Work leaped to the top of his priority list when he saw Jake Lovejoy approaching as if he were the wrath of God about to descend on Judd. The owner was a silver-haired man who spent enough time at the gym that he looked at least ten years younger than his true age of sixty. Judd figured Lovejoy could bench-press two hundred pounds and might be able to take Judd in a fight. The team owner's scowl indicated he would like nothing better than to exchange a few punches with his crew chief.

Lovejoy jerked his head in the direction of the door. Putting on his sunglasses, he walked out on the tarmac. Judd tugged the brim of his cap down, took a deep breath, and followed him. Today would be a bad day to get fired.

Stopping outside the door, Lovejoy turned, his eyes hidden behind his glasses. "Hell's bells, son! You were supposed to make nice with Merritt on that show!"

Judd wished he could see past those damned mirrored shades. "I said he was a talented driver."

"Yeah, and then you said the jury was out as to whether he's become too arrogant to be coachable."

"I don't believe I said all that, and I know I didn't use the word *arrogant*."

Lovejoy waved a hand dismissively. "Doesn't matter. I understood the implication, and so did Merritt. So did the fans, but more important, so did the sponsor."

"Sorry about that, Mr. Lovejoy. I'm not a good liar."

"We'll all be sorry if this thing doesn't settle down. Goddess Chocolates isn't happy." He held up his thumb and forefinger so they were almost touching. "They're this close to dropping us."

"I apologize, sir. I should have been more complimentary to Merritt and taken the fifth on that direct question."

"That wouldn't have helped. Once you were in that quagmire, you had no way out." He lowered his voice. "Is it true? Is Merritt too full of himself to run a good race?"

This was the first time Judd had heard Lovejoy voice the slightest doubt about his favorite driver. Judd had always assumed if one of them had to go, it would be him and not Merritt. He was sobered by the possibility that he could throw the balance in the other direction by whatever he chose to say to Lovejoy.

And he knew what that had to be. The day before the biggest race of the year, Lovejoy needed to have confidence in his driver. "Merritt's a pro," Judd said. "Once he's out there, he won't be thinking about anything but getting to Victory Lane. I can't promise you or Goddess Chocolates that we'll accomplish that, but I can promise an all-out effort."

Lovejoy nodded. "You're one hell of a crew chief, Timmons. And Merritt's an exciting driver. I'd appreciate it if the two of you could present a more united front. I don't like the team being the subject of rumors. And that's putting it mildly."

Judd thought about Roni's effort to fix the problem. She'd been more loyal to the team than either Judd or Tucker. "I'll see that this gets worked out," he said.

"Thanks." Lovejoy stuck out his hand. "I'm counting on you."

"I won't let you down." Judd returned to the garage with a new sense of purpose. Lovejoy was counting on him to be the mature adult in this situation, and Judd couldn't say that he'd acted like one. He'd allowed himself to make a derogatory comment about Merritt in the interview.

Deep down, he'd felt justified because he'd been forced to do the interview and because he considered Merritt in the wrong. He'd had no intention of cutting Merritt any slack until the guy apologized.

Merritt might never apologize, and Judd had to be okay with that. Building a cohesive racing team was more important than repairing his damaged pride, and it was time for him to realize it.

Before he could make it back over to the car, Orville stopped him and leaned close enough to be heard over the noise. "I saw you with Lovejoy. After I watched the interview I thought he might show up this morning."

"Yeah, he wasn't happy. But it'll be okay. I know what I have to do."

Orville's eyebrows rose. "Is that right? And what's the magic formula?"

"Swallow my pride and get on with winning races."

"I like it." Orville clapped him on the back. "Speaking of that, do we have a new car chief?"

Judd blinked. She'd never officially accepted the car chief's job. Come to think of it, he wasn't sure if he'd officially asked her. He'd mentioned it, and then the subject had been dropped.

He wasn't willing to explain all that to Orville. "She's thinking it over," he said.

"Really? I expected her to jump on it. She loves her job and I sense that she's ambitious. That position will look good on her résumé, whether she stays with us or not."

Judd rebelled at the idea of Roni leaving the team. He didn't want her going anywhere. "I think she'll take it."

"Good."

"Yeah, I'm sure she'll take it." He felt like an idiot. Obviously he was terrible at mixing business with pleasure.

"Did you talk about money?" Orville asked.

"Uh, not yet."

"Good grief, Judd. What *did* you talk about?"

Now there was a question Judd could answer. "She told me her story. You had suggested I ask her about it, so I did. I heard all about the Last Chance Ranch."

"I see." Orville's gaze was speculative.

"It's good to know the background of the people you work with every day."

"I absolutely agree." Something on the far side of the garage caught Orville's attention. "It's inspection time. We need to get over there. Let me know when she takes the job."

"Don't worry. I will." And Judd planned to ask Roni about it first chance he got. He wanted her in the war wagon with him tomorrow during the race, and as car chief, she'd have every right to be there.

ORDINARILY RONI LOVED the frantic pace of Saturday, with its tight schedule of inspections, media appearances for the driver, and the final practice before the race the next day. It was all part of building the excitement that would crescendo tomorrow afternoon when the green flag dropped. But today she would have appreciated a few minutes to speak with Judd.

As for Tucker, he spent the morning practice complaining about the car. Roni guessed that Tucker's foul mood was directly connected to last night, and he was taking out his anger on Judd and the rest of the hapless team, including her. Nevertheless, it was her job to make the driver happy with the car's setup, so she worked with the pit crew as they struggled to shave off another second from the lap time.

She had to hand it to Judd. He was extremely patient with Tucker. He made a point of calling him by his first name, something he used to do before they'd had their falling out. Tucker, however, refused to use Judd's affectionate nickname of Iceman. If he called Judd by name at all, it was simply *Timmons*.

Minute by torturous minute, Roni expected Judd to lose it. It had happened several times at the end of last season and a few times this year in the preseason.

But not today. Apparently Judd had finally realized the serious nature of this rift, even though Tucker didn't seem to have a clue. It was bad enough that crew members could pick up on Tucker's complaints on their headsets, but come race day, any fan wearing a headset could do the same. Fans could now tune in to the frequency used by their favorite driver and crew chief. No wonder the sponsor didn't want angry words flying between Tucker and Judd.

On Tucker's final practice lap, he kept up a steady stream of negativity, as if trying to goad Judd into responding in kind. "This car handles like a supermarket shopping buggy," he said as he pulled into the pit for the final time.

Judd glanced over at Roni and rolled his eyes. She laughed, and it was the shiniest moment of the morning so far.

"That means you'll get extra credit when you bring this shopping buggy into Victory Lane, Tucker." Judd pulled off his headset and motioned to Roni.

Leaving the rest of the crew to deal with the car and Tucker, Roni followed Judd to a far corner of the garage. The noise level was still intense, and people were everywhere, but Roni felt as if they were enclosed in a cocoon of intimacy.

He didn't touch her, but the sparkle of awareness in his blue eyes made up for the lack of physical contact. "You were great," he said.

"You, too. As for Tucker, not so much."

"I noticed." Judd took off his Goddess Chocolates cap and tunneled his fingers through his hair. "We need to get him to meet with us tonight. If he'll let you talk to him, say whatever you need to—tell him I'm ready to admit I was in the wrong and that I believe he didn't sleep with Loretta. Tell him I want a chance to apologize."

"Judd! You shouldn't have to grovel. He's being a total—"

"Doesn't matter." His gaze searched hers. "Will you tell him? I would, but I think there's a better chance he'll listen to you."

"He's not so happy with me at the moment, either."

"No, but I don't think he'll completely blow you off, and we need to try whatever we can for the team's sake. I had a talk with Lovejoy this morning."

"Guess I missed that." Roni did her best to focus on the subject at hand and not stare at Judd's kissable mouth.

"Lovejoy's having doubts about Tucker. The kid's too young and inexperienced to realize how his temper tantrums are hurting him. Lovejoy's not likely to fire him now, at the beginning of the season, but if his behavior causes the sponsor to bail, then all bets are off. Even if he doesn't fire him, he could make his life a living hell and team morale will get even worse."

"What about you?" Roni's tummy churned at the thought of Judd's career in jeopardy.

"I doubt Lovejoy would fire me at this point in the season, either, but he could make us all really miserable. A miserable team won't win many races. I wish I could take back what I said on TV. I didn't know my opinion carried such weight with Lovejoy, or I would have tried harder to keep my mouth shut."

Roni laid her hand on Judd's arm. "You didn't want to do the interview at all, remember? Lovejoy's the one who insisted."

He glanced down at her hand. "Roni…"

She jerked her hand away. "Whoops."

"You have no idea what that one little touch does to me."

Her heart beat faster. "Really?"

"Yeah." He took a breath. "And we both have to get moving. The car's due for another inspection."

"Do you want me to be there?"

"I'd rather have you go find Tucker."

"Okay. I'll let you know what he says." She started to walk away.

"Roni?"

"Yes?"

"I never officially offered you the job of car chief. I'm offering it now. Will you take it? I'd like to announce the news to the crew this afternoon."

The word *yes* was nearly out of her mouth when she stopped herself from saying it. She'd vowed when she chose this profession that she wouldn't allow anyone to pay her less because of her gender. She definitely couldn't allow her feelings for Judd to influence her career decisions. Consequently, she made herself ask the right question. "What are you willing to pay?"

He smiled. "Attagirl."

"I wouldn't want you to think I'm a pushover."

"Any woman who's capable of hot-wiring a truck and attempting to steal it out from under the noses of trail-hardened cowboys is no pushover."

"So, how much?"

He named a figure.

"I think you can do better than that."

He attempted a scowl, but he obviously couldn't manage it and started to laugh. "With your attitude, you'll be one hell of a car chief. How about if I raise that amount by ten percent?"

"Done."

"Let's hope the team is prosperous this season, so that ten percent means something."

"It will be prosperous," Roni said. "We're going to fix this, Judd. Together."

"I do believe we are." His gaze was warm, and he seemed about to say something, but then he shook his head. "I'm glad you're taking the job."

"So am I." Maybe she was a fool for agreeing to work closely with Judd when he'd made it clear he didn't want a personal relationship. Maybe she'd end up with a broken heart. Then again, maybe the Iceman would thaw.

RONI FOUND TUCKER AT the temporary gym frequented by drivers and any other racing personnel. Earbuds in and iPod clipped to his gym shorts, Tucker was using one of the treadmills. He glanced sideways as she approached, but then he faced forward again and kept going.

Fortunately only one other person, a driver named Anderson Blaycock, was in the gym. He was on the far side of the room on the weight machine and was also using an iPod. She hoped he wouldn't be able to hear her, but she couldn't do much about that.

Suggesting that Judd wanted a chance to apologize didn't sit well with her, but she needed a dramatic opening or Tucker would ignore her. She knew exactly how he'd react because once upon a time her attitude toward any authority figure had been exactly like his.

She thought back to the belligerent teenager who'd been fearlessly hitchhiking that Wyoming country road. Tucker wasn't a teenager, but his mental age might not be too far beyond that. She remembered thinking that the world owed her something after all she'd been through, which was why she'd felt entitled to steal a truck from her benefactors.

Much as it rubbed her wrong, she'd have to go with Judd's offer of an apology. "Tucker, Judd asked me to tell you—"

"I have to listen to him on the track, but I don't have to off the track, and I don't intend to."

She fought the urge to grab him by the scruff of the neck and give him a shake. "Judd wants to apologize."

"Oh, really?"

"Yes, really. Let's try again. Come by my room tonight around six. It'll be a neutral zone."

Tucker's laugh was bitter. "Neutral? I don't think so. It's more like two against one. And I used to think you were on *my* side."

"I'm not on any side." Except that wasn't strictly true anymore. If Tucker and Judd were both drowning, she'd choose to save Judd over Tucker. But in this case, she might be able to save them both.

Tucker wiped his face with a towel and kept walking. "Oh, I think you're on a side. You don't give a crap about me. You're pushing this for Timmons's sake."

"Actually, I can't afford to let either one of you fail. The sponsor's threatened to drop us, and if that happens, we're all in trouble. Judd's made me car chief, and if I was loyal to this team before, I'm even more so, now."

Tucker looked at her. "Car chief, huh? Congratulations."

She ignored his sarcasm. "Thank you."

"FYI, don't sweat the problems with the sponsor. I'll sweet-talk them on Sunday at the meet-and-greet, and we'll all be fine. You've been a good friend, at least until you joined the Judd Timmons fan club, so I'll watch out for you."

If so much hadn't been at stake, she would have found his cockiness funny. "I hope you have a silver tongue on Sunday, then."

"I will." Tucker grabbed a water bottle from a holder on the treadmill and drank as he continued logging miles.

"You'll definitely need it. From what I hear, the sponsor is very unhappy with this battle between you and Judd. In case you hadn't noticed, Judd's laid down his weapons. He let every one of your snarky comments during practice go unchallenged."

"Too bad he wasn't of that frame of mind during the TV interview."

"He agrees. He's sorry about those comments he made and wants to apologize in person. He wants to get past this. If you refuse, that makes you the troublemaker."

Tucker paced silently for a while. "I might come by your room tonight and I might not."

Roni tried not to get her hopes up, but she glimpsed a crack in his armor. "I hope you do. The whole team will benefit if you iron things out."

"I'm glad you mentioned the team. It's all well and good if Timmons wants to apologize to me in the privacy of your hotel room. That won't change the fact that most of the crew is convinced I slept with his girlfriend. I want him to tell everybody I didn't. Either he agrees to do that or there's no point to any of this."

Roni closed her eyes in frustration. Judd was such a private man, such a proud man. A private apology he shouldn't have to make was one thing, but to make a public one...she didn't see it happening.

She didn't dare say that. "I'll talk to Judd about your condition."

"No, let me do that. He won't go for it, but it will be fun watching you try to convince him he should."

"Are you saying you'll come, then?" This could all be for nothing, because she agreed with him about Judd's reaction to a public apology for his actions.

"I will if you promise not to spill the beans about my one condition. I want the pleasure of seeing his face when I bring that up."

She hesitated.

"Up to you. I don't have to show at all." He took another long swig of water as he continued to walk.

"All right, I won't tell him about your extra provision." She tried to convince herself it would be okay because she'd be there to referee. Maybe a miracle would happen in her room tonight and the two men would dig deep enough to find their former friendship. Maybe Tucker would relent and not demand that public apology. She prayed that would be the case.

"Then I'll be there," Tucker said.

"Thank you." Roni left the gym before he could dream up any more conditions.

Once on her way back to the garage, she pulled her BlackBerry from the pocket of her uniform and texted Judd. This was something she'd rather put in a message than tell him face-to-face. She'd see him again in a few moments, but she'd rather not talk about this impending meeting. The less she talked about it with Judd, the less guilty she'd feel about the devil's bargain she'd made with Tucker.

CHAPTER SIX

JUDD AND THE CREW WERE in the middle of the inspection process when Roni showed up. He waited until the car had passed the final phase in the seemingly endless round of inspections. Then he gathered the crew so he could announce that Roni was the team's new car chief.

Judd was gratified that his announcement was greeted with applause. He glanced over at Roni and his heart swelled at her bright smile of joy.

Later he took her aside. "That went well."

Her green eyes shone with pride. "It's very cool that the crew is behind me."

"They should be. You're a top-notch mechanic." He paused. "Did you locate Tucker?"

"I did. Didn't you get my text? He's coming."

"Do you think he—"

"I texted you the details. Thought it would be safer. Listen, if the weather holds, I'm thinking we might short-pit for the last stop tomorrow."

"It's a gamble either way," Judd said. "The car goes faster on four new tires."

"But we gain time by only replacing two."

"Unless the pit crew can pick up a second or two with their tire changes. And I think they're capable of it." As Judd became engrossed in discussing race day strategy with Roni, he forgot about her text message.

He didn't remember it until he was back in his hotel room, taking off his clothes in preparation for hopping in the shower. The details from Roni were uncomplicated. Tucker would be at her hotel at six. Judd planned to get there a little earlier than that.

He didn't look forward to the meeting, but he'd do what he had to do. This had gone on long enough, and if he had to eat some crow in order to put an end to it, he'd do that.

There was a second message, this one from Anderson Blaycock asking Judd to call him ASAP. Andy had been driving for nearly ten years and the guy had racked up quite a few trips to Victory Lane. He had a pretty blond wife named Suzanne and two adorable blond kids, a boy about six and a girl about three. Maybe they were older now. Judd tended to lose track.

He didn't know Andy well, but he respected the guy. He had a reputation as a straight shooter, popular with both the fans and the other drivers. Judd had no idea why Andy would be contacting him, but an urgent message from a driver the night before a major race required a response.

Keeping an eye on the clock, he punched in Andy's number.

Andy picked up immediately. "Hey, Judd. I was hoping to hear from you before I headed out for dinner."

"I just noticed the message. What's up?"

On the other end, Andy hesitated. "This is a sensitive subject, but I know I can trust you not to spread any gossip."

"Absolutely." Judd's curiosity was aroused, and although the clock was ticking, he wasn't about to say that to Andy. The man sounded as if he had to weigh every word.

"It's about Loretta Sinclair."

A chill ran down Judd's spine. "She's okay, I hope?"

"She's fine. Loretta's always fine. It's the people she leaves in her wake who end up capsizing."

"I'm not sure what you mean. Do you know her?"

Andy laughed softly. "I know her, but fortunately not in the Biblical sense. She tried to make that happen, but I shut her down. I love my wife. Thank God she loves me and trusts me, because Loretta tried to convince Suzanne that I was a liar and a cheat."

"She tried to break up your marriage?" Judd thought about Loretta, her big violet eyes filled with tears, her full lips trembling. She'd always seemed young and vulnerable to Judd.

"Yep, that's exactly what she tried to do. I'd

bruised her ego by rejecting her, so for revenge she went to see Suzanne and made up a story about me seducing her."

"When was this?" Judd was thinking it might be several years ago, when Loretta was younger and more foolish.

"The beginning of last season."

"And what happened?"

"Suzanne, true-blue woman that she is, refused to believe it. I'm convinced Loretta would have gone to the media next, except that Suzanne anticipated that and called our lawyer, who contacted Loretta and laid out precisely what would happen to her if she engaged in that kind of character assassination."

"Incredible." Judd paced the hotel room and ran his fingers through his already tousled hair. "I started dating her at the end of March, and she never said a word about this."

"That's because the lawyer put the fear of God in her. But I've left out the most important part. Before she came on to me, she'd been dating Bob Jansen, my crew chief. I'm convinced he was only a stepping stone. You know the type—a woman who dates a crew member to get to the driver."

"I know the type. I just didn't…" A queasy sensation invaded his gut.

"She puts on one helluva show, buddy."

"That's no excuse." Judd felt like six kinds of a fool. Sure, he knew that kind of groupie existed, but he hadn't seen the pattern in Loretta. She'd been so damned convincing when she'd claimed to care about Judd. She'd been even more believable when she'd insisted that Tucker had approached her.

"I've wanted to say something to you for months." Andy sighed. "But like a coward, I hesitated. I'd ducked a potential scandal, and I didn't want to take a chance that by talking to you, I'd stir Loretta up again. Then I heard Roni arguing with Tucker in the gym and knew I had to say something. Loretta's poison, man."

Judd closed his eyes and took a deep breath. "I appreciate the heads-up."

"I'm afraid it's a day late and a dollar short. Sorry, Judd. You might want to ask Tucker what she said to him. Odds are she told him you were out to ruin him. That's her style, to sow discord when she doesn't get what she wants. Anyway, I gotta go. I'm meeting some people. But I'm glad we connected."

"Andy, I'm grateful. I owe you."

"Hey, buy me a beer sometime. And I really hope you and Tucker work this out. I hate what she's done to your team. See you around, man."

"Later, Andy." Judd ended the call and sank to the end of the bed, the BlackBerry still in his hand as he stared into space. He'd thought his apology to Tucker would be bogus, a bone he was throwing Tucker's way so the kid would forget their feud and get on with the business of racing.

It turned out that he really did owe Tucker an

apology. No wonder the young driver was so combative. Nothing stirred a person's blood more than being unjustly accused, especially if the accuser was someone you liked and respected.

The sick feeling in the pit of his stomach hardened into a fist of anger. Loretta had a lot to answer for. He should find her, confront her, make her… make her do what?

In order to prove anything, he'd have to repeat Andy's story, as well as his own, and he'd pledged to keep Andy out of this. One sleazy bit of behavior didn't constitute a pattern. Frustration tightened his jaw, but at last he had to acknowledge that he had no way to fight her.

He could, however, work to repair the damage she'd caused. And as they said, living well was the best revenge.

RONI HAD EXPECTED JUDD to show up early, but instead Tucker was the first to arrive. He was dressed in the current style Roni had seen in magazines—shirttail hanging out over his jeans and a gold brocade vest that made him look like an Old West gambling man. She supposed the image fit Tucker, who gambled every time he climbed into the No. 414 car.

It was a calculated risk, though, because he had a fair idea of how to play the game. She, on the other hand, had invited these two feuding men to her hotel room with no real concept of how to play this game. She hoped to get some inspiration fast.

Tucker glanced into the room as he came through the door. "I thought Timmons was going to be here."

"He should be here any minute."

Walking into the room, Tucker chose one of the chairs by the curtained window. He sat in typical Tucker fashion, sprawled in the chair, legs spread, taking up space. "Maybe he chickened out."

She opened her mouth to defend Judd, but that wouldn't help the mood between her and Tucker. Because he was here first, she had a chance to change his mind about his plan to have Judd publicly humiliate himself.

"Maybe he did chicken out," she said. "But I think he'll be here."

Tucker's gaze flicked over her. "You never dressed up like that for me."

"Tucker, I never dressed up like this for anybody."

"So why the change?"

"I figured out that I would never get Judd's attention if I stuck with my tomboy routine."

Tucker's eyes narrowed. "Seriously? This is all for Timmons?"

"Don't pretend you don't know that I've had a crush on him ever since I came to work for Lovejoy. The rest of the crew knows, so I'm sure you've drawn the same conclusion."

"Yeah, I suppose I knew on some level." He laced

his fingers over his flat stomach. "Maybe I was hoping you'd get over it. Anyway, you look good." He delivered the compliment grudgingly.

"Thank you." She'd worn snug blue jeans, a black vee-necked sweater and silver drop earrings. She'd left her hair down, but had decided against an elaborate blow-dry and styling gel. Instead, her freshly washed hair fell in soft layers, framing her face and reaching just to her shoulders.

Tucker's gaze turned speculative. "So how's it going? Have you two hooked up?"

"Not exactly." She sat on the end of the bed so she was facing him.

Tucker steepled his fingers and tapped them against his chin. "I'll bet Timmons is nervous about dating a crew member. Now that you're the car chief, he'll be even more paranoid about it."

Roni feared that was true. By taking the car chief's job, she might have erected one more barrier between her and Judd. "He's not paranoid," she said. "He's cautious. He puts the team's welfare first."

"I hope you're right. I put my life on the line every time I go out."

"You can trust Judd." If she was certain of nothing else, she was certain of that.

"At this point, I have to trust him, don't I?"

In that brief moment she glimpsed the scared kid hiding behind Tucker's bad-boy bravado. He was only twenty-four and in a pressure cooker of a profession. That could be exhilarating when you had support and terrifying when you didn't. No wonder he'd been acting like a jerk. He wasn't sure who he could count on.

A knock sounded at the door, and Tucker's relaxed pose changed. He scooted back in the chair and gripped the arms, as if needing something to hold on to. Roni mentally crossed her fingers as she went to answer the door.

CHAPTER SEVEN

JUDD DETESTED BEING LATE, but his phone call to Andy had put him behind. He wondered if Tucker would already be there when he arrived. On the way over, he'd rehearsed what he planned to say and had reminded himself that he wanted to use Tucker's first name at all times to make the discussion more personal.

Everything went out of his head when Roni opened the door. Tight black sweaters were made for this woman. His mouth went dry as he stared at her.

The blue silk had been tough to resist, but this black sweater sent off sirens in his brain and awakened parts of him that needed to behave.

Her lemon scent reached out to him, daring him to take her in his arms and to hell with his private code of conduct. He'd thought his soft moan of delight had been internal, but obviously not, because her eyebrows lifted.

"Are you okay?" she asked softly.

He cleared his throat. "I'm fine."

"Tucker's already here."

Judd glanced past her and saw Merritt sitting in the same chair Judd had occupied the night before. He had been so engrossed by the sight of Roni that an elephant could have been standing in the room and he'd never have noticed until she pointed it out.

"Sorry I'm late," he said. "But it was in a good cause."

"Glad to hear it." Her green eyes held his for a moment longer. Then she stepped aside. "Come in."

Tucker stood as Judd walked into the room. Judd took it more as an offensive maneuver than a gesture of respect. No guy wanted to get into an argument while he was sitting down and the other man was standing. Judd would do everything he could to prevent an argument, but he couldn't guarantee anything.

He was a couple of inches taller than Tucker, although that had never seemed to matter before. When he noticed Tucker balancing on the balls of his feet, he realized it mattered tonight. Tucker was poised like a prize fighter. Judd's goal was to avoid exchanging punches.

For his opening gambit, he stuck out his hand. "Thanks for coming."

Tucker met his gaze and left both hands at his sides.

So that's how it was going to be. No pleasantries, no pretense of civilized behavior. Judd slowly lowered his hand but kept eye contact with Tucker. Neither of them seemed inclined to blink.

"Why don't you both sit down?" Roni said. "Now

that everyone's here, I could order something from room service. What would you each like?"

"Nothing for me," Tucker said.

"Not for me, either, thanks. We might as well get to it. Tucker, I owe you a huge apology."

"It sure took you long enough, Timmons."

Roni gasped. "Tucker! Could you be even a little bit gracious about this?"

"Why should I be? My reputation's been dragged through the mud ever since October, while this guy is beloved. Do you have any idea how that feels, Timmons? If I had a dollar for every dirty look sent my way in the past few months, I could retire from racing."

Judd's voice was tight. "I'm truly sorry for that, but everyone thought you'd slept with Loretta."

"Correction." Tucker pointed an accusing finger at Judd. "Everyone thought I *seduced* Loretta, stole her right out from under your nose and then dumped her. Does that about sum it up?"

"We were all wrong. I was wrong."

"Damn straight you were wrong! But why are you conveniently coming to that conclusion right now? Because Lovejoy's breathing down your neck? Worried about your precious job, Timmons?"

"He's breathing down both our necks, Merritt! If you'd just shut up and listen for two seconds, I think you'd find the experience enlightening."

"Judd." Roni laid a hand on his arm.

Judd gritted his teeth. He'd done what he'd vowed not to do. He'd lost his temper and he'd used Tucker's last name. Considering what Andy had revealed, Tucker deserved Judd's best effort to keep the peace.

"Oh, don't stop him now, Roni," Tucker said. "He's just building up a good head of steam. Let's find out what the real Judd Timmons is all about."

"He's about building a better relationship between you two," Roni said. "Right, Judd?"

"Right." He stabbed his fingers through his hair and glanced at Tucker. "I learned something today, and I can't divulge my source because I promised not to. But it looks like Loretta set up both of us. I suggest we compare stories, because I have reason to believe she was playing us against each other."

Tucker looked wary. "Why would she do that? I don't see any motivation."

"For power. For revenge. Let's say she hooked up with me as a way to eventually land the ultimate prize—you. We both know that happens in this business."

"I guess." Tucker's jaw relaxed a fraction.

Judd thought he might have softened Tucker up a bit by calling him the ultimate prize. Whatever worked was fine with him. "Let's say she made a play for you, and you rejected her."

"Which I did. You don't believe that, but—"

"That's just it," Judd said. "I do believe you, and I should have seen through her story from the beginning. My only excuse is that Loretta's an accomplished actress. She put on a convincing show."

Tucker nodded as more of his belligerence slipped away. "So consequently you hated my guts."

"Pretty much."

"And then Loretta comes to me again." Tucker was obviously warming to the subject. "She says to watch out for you. She says you're jealous of my success because you washed out as a driver."

Judd stared at him. "She said that?"

"Yeah, pal, she said that. She said you wanted me to fail."

"Good God." The puzzle clicked into place for Judd. "And there you have her motivation. She didn't get what she wanted, which was to hook up with you, so she decided to drag us both down."

Tucker gazed at him, his expression tightening again. "And I've been through months of hell because you believed her instead of me."

"She was crying. She seemed heartbroken. I—"

"You didn't trust me. You thought I was capable of sleeping with my crew chief's girlfriend."

"Tucker, you always have women around you. You're only twenty-four. It seemed perfectly plaus—"

"Being young and popular with women doesn't mean I have no sense of loyalty! Damn you, Timmons, for not having more faith in me!"

Judd was stunned into silence by the realization that Tucker was absolutely right. He couldn't look at Roni, because he was afraid he'd see the same dawning comprehension in her expression.

But before he drowned in guilt, he needed to remember that he wasn't the only one who'd lacked trust. "It cuts both ways," he said. "If you'd had more faith in me, you'd know I would never sabotage your career. You'd have laughed in Loretta's face when she made that accusation. Looks as if both of us have been short on trust, doesn't it?"

"If we have, I'm the one who's paid the biggest price. You want to fix this thing between us? Here's how you do it. Tomorrow before the race, you get the whole crew together and tell them you misjudged my character and that you now realize I didn't seduce your girlfriend. You say that I am, and always have been, a loyal member of the Lovejoy team."

Judd cringed at the idea. It was so not his way of operating. But what choice did he have? Tucker had been wrongly accused, and he was the only one who could set things right again.

"Don't want to do it, do you, Timmons?" Tucker rocked back on his heels. "That's right. You're the Iceman. You want everything cool and businesslike. A great girl like Roni might be interested in you, but you aren't about to take that risk, either, because it might disturb the calm surface of your life."

Judd fought to hold on to his temper. "Now *that* is really none of your business."

Roni stepped forward. "Tucker, let's not get into my relationship with Judd. We have enough to handle with this Loretta situation without—"

"It's all tied together," Tucker said. "There's nothing wrong with Judd letting the team know he's human, that he makes mistakes and that he's falling for the team's car chief. I say he needs to—"

"I'll do it, Tucker."

Roni's eyes widened. "Do what? Which?"

"Call the team meeting and admit I judged Tucker unfairly. As for the situation between you and me, that's for us to decide, not Tucker."

"I agree," Roni said.

Tucker raised both hands. "Whatever. So, are we done, here? I have things to do."

"We're done." Judd dreaded what he'd just agreed to, but if that's what would make Tucker feel less victimized, then that's what Judd would do.

"Tucker," Roni said. "Hold on a minute. Maybe Judd could talk to each of the crew members individually instead of at a team meeting."

Tucker shook his head. "That would have way less impact."

"Let it go, Roni," Judd said. "I'll hold the team meeting. It's the right thing to do."

"I'll be waiting for that golden moment." Tucker started out the door, but turned back. "Just be glad I'm not asking you to call a press conference. The idea did cross my mind." Then he was gone.

Roni glanced over at Judd, wanting to offer support, not sure if he would welcome it. He stood, hands on his hips, and studied the carpet as if searching for inspiration in the gold and green geometric pattern at his feet. She'd been the one to initiate the meeting between Judd and Tucker, but it had spiraled completely out of her control.

Finally Judd looked up, his expression bleak. "So that's it, then."

"I can only imagine what it will cost you to hold that team meeting. I'm sorry."

"It is what it is. I hate that expression, but in this case, it fits."

"The person who should be addressing the team meeting is Loretta." Roni's anger bubbled back to the surface. "I'd really like to get her alone in a back alley and clean her clock. She gives women a bad name."

"I know. I wish I could post a warning about her somewhere, but it could come across as gossip or even worse, revenge."

"Yes, it would. You'd be better off rising above it, unless, of course, you see her going after another team."

"You can bet I'll be watching."

Roni nodded. "That makes two of us."

"But even if I can blame Loretta for starting the rumor, the truth is I did nothing to stop it from spreading. I allowed the crew to think whatever they wanted, and most of them think I'm the good guy and Tucker is the snake in the grass."

"I wish he'd agreed to let you spread the word gradually, though."

Judd sighed. "No, Tucker's right. The team meeting will have a greater impact, bring about the change faster. And it beats the hell out of a press conference."

"True." Roni couldn't even imagine that, given Judd's feelings about media appearances.

"I think Tucker enjoyed throwing out that last zinger."

She rolled her eyes. "Yes, he certainly did. You may hate drama, but he loves it."

Judd studied her silently for a moment. "Do you love it?"

The question caught her by surprise. "I'm not sure what you mean."

"I've been thinking back over what you told me about your background. Leaving home by hitchhiking was pretty dramatic. Stealing the truck was, too, and then there were those impromptu drag races on the ranch."

"I suppose." His evaluation made her a little nervous. Maybe she shouldn't have painted herself as such a wild child. She didn't want to be lumped into the same category as Tucker.

"Then there's your new look." His gaze traveled over her with such warmth that she blushed. "That's definitely dramatic."

"Judd, I'm not a drama queen, if that's what you're getting at."

"No, I'm not saying that at all. Nobody who's watched your steady work the past couple of years could ever say that. You're exciting and fun, but you're no drama queen."

Exciting and fun. That sounded promising. So maybe he wasn't comparing her behavior with Tucker's. "What are you asking, then?"

"Whether or not you're into grand gestures. It's something a guy needs to know about the woman he's involved with."

Her heartbeat slammed into high gear. "But we're not involved, Judd."

He crossed to her and cupped her face in both hands. "We're about to be."

Liquid heat poured through her. "But…you don't think it's wise."

"It's not." He caressed her cheeks with his thumbs as he gazed into her eyes. "But Tucker's right. Only a fool would pass up a chance to be with you. So tell me, are you into grand gestures?"

She gulped. "Right now I'd settle for a small, private gesture."

"Such as?"

"A kiss."

His mouth drifted closer to hers. "We haven't had dinner."

"Dinner can wait." She was hungry for something much more interesting than food. Her body thrummed with anticipation.

His eyes darkened. "Room service in a couple of hours?"

"Exactly." It was the last coherent word she spoke.

Later, as they lay warm and sated amid the tumbled sheets of her king-size bed, she gazed into his eyes. Unable to hold back a smile of pure joy, she leaned toward him and placed a soft kiss on his beautiful mouth. "Now that," she said, "was what I would call a grand gesture."

CHAPTER EIGHT

JUDD SPENT MOST OF the night with Roni, which meant he wasn't particularly rested by the time he arrived at the track the next morning. As if he cared. He'd never lost sleep with so much pleasure.

He'd always wondered if he'd recognize the right woman when she came along. Now he knew the answer. From the day he'd met Roni, everything had clicked, but he hadn't allowed himself to see it. She'd had to hit him over the head, just as Derek had told her to.

When Judd arrived at the track, racing fever was thick in the air. By race time, the grandstands would be filled to capacity with fans who were on hand to witness a legendary race, the Super Bowl of NASCAR. Adrenaline rushed through him, as it always did on this first Sunday of the season.

But before he allowed himself to be swept up in the excitement, he had an important item to handle. Pulling out his BlackBerry, he called one of his connections at Goddess Chocolates. Roni had never answered his question about grand gestures, but he'd reached his own conclusion.

Thank God he'd looked at his BlackBerry before clipping it to his belt this morning. He'd been checking for any messages he might have missed while he was in the shower, but in the process he'd noticed the date. February 14. If a guy didn't make a grand gesture on February 14, he might never get another chance.

He was about to clip the BlackBerry to his belt again and head into the garage when Lovejoy's ring came through loud and clear. Judd felt calm about talking to Lovejoy today. After all, he was doing everything he could to solve the problem.

"Just wanted to give you a heads-up," Lovejoy said. "You're scheduled for a live TV interview today with Stan Baker before the race."

Judd stifled a groan. He was in no position to argue. "Just me, or is Tucker supposed to be there?"

"Just you. After the drivers' meeting. He'll find you."

"I'll be watching for him."

"And think about what you say this time."

"I will." Judd planned to think very carefully about what he said. He wouldn't allow another interviewer to trip him up.

"Good luck today, Timmons."

Judd thanked him and they ended the connection. Another interview. Oh, joy. But even that couldn't ruin his happiness. It was race day. It was Valentine's Day. He was in love with Roni Kenway. It was all good.

FOR THE FIRST TIME SINCE Roni joined the Lovejoy team, the race wasn't her primary concern, and that was bad now that she was the car chief. As she suited up and headed over to the No. 414 car, another 14 was on her mind, February 14, to be exact.

After an incredible night with Judd, she still didn't know where she stood with him. Oh, they were having an affair. That much was very clear. Any man who'd enjoyed himself as much as Judd had seemed to would be coming back for more.

This morning he'd kissed her with enthusiasm and passion before leaving her room, but any mention of Valentine's Day had been conspicuously absent. She wondered if he even knew it was today. He could certainly be forgiven on that score, considering all he had on his mind, but still…

Might as well face it. She wanted him to acknowledge that they had something special. To her great surprise, she had a sentimental streak a mile wide, and she wanted the guy she was in love with to wish her a Happy Valentine's Day. She couldn't reasonably expect him to be in love with her yet, but in lust was good enough for now.

Maybe that was the rub. He might consider anything Valentine-related as evidence of a commitment he wasn't willing to make, at least not yet. She'd had two years to fantasize about a relationship. He'd only had two days. She was expecting too much. She should be happy with what she had, and she was. She *was*.

With a sigh, she cancelled any plans to acknowledge this special day, which was just as well. She didn't have time to shop for a card, let alone a gift. But if he'd simply said *Happy Valentine's Day* this morning, she would have figured out something. But he hadn't mentioned the holiday.

At that moment the object of her affections walked into the garage from the direction of the infield. When he spotted her, his smile made her forget all her Valentine angst. He'd smiled at her before in the two years they'd known each other, but this morning he'd boosted the wattage at least a hundred percent, leaving no doubt that he was really glad to see her. She answered that smile with one of equal delight.

Because it was race day, she'd given up all pretense of glamour, wearing her hair in its usual ponytail and a minimum of makeup. It didn't seem to matter to Judd. His pace quickened as if he longed to swing her up into his arms and spin her around the way men did in the movies.

As they walked toward each other, she imagined them moving in slow motion with a syrupy theme song playing in the background. Surely anyone watching would recognize that they were sleeping together.

When he was only a few feet away, she spoke. "Better wipe that grin off your face."

He laughed. "I will if you will."

"Can't do it."

"Me, either."

She decided this was way better than a silly old Valentine's Day card. Apparently he didn't care if anyone knew about their relationship. "But people will talk."

"Nah. They're all so focused on the race they couldn't care less if we smile a lot."

Oh. So maybe he wanted to keep their involvement secret but wasn't worried about attracting attention on race day, when everyone was preoccupied. Her happiness dimmed a little. Not a lot, but a little.

"Something wrong?"

She jacked up her smile again. "Absolutely not. Everything's perfect."

"I hope so." His gaze held hers. "Everything sure was perfect last night."

The heat of that glance made her tingle in all the places he'd paid such devoted attention to only hours ago. "Yeah," she said softly. "It was." And it would be again tonight, and the night after that.

Chances were he'd go public with their relationship eventually, but she had to be patient. She needed to remember this was the Iceman, a person who liked to keep his private business to himself.

He groaned softly. "Roni, I swear, if I stand here another second, I'll kiss you."

"We can't have that." She thought it would be a brilliant move, but he obviously didn't want to give in to the impulse. "Anyway, it's time to get the car through the inspection line."

"Yeah. But before we go over there, let me warn you that Lovejoy's turned the media loose on me again. A TV crew will show up for an interview with me sometime between the end of the drivers' meeting and the start of the race."

"That sucks."

He chuckled. "Well put."

"I mean, aside from the fact you hate interviews, the timing is terrible. What can he be thinking?"

"I'm guessing that the sponsor wants to improve the team's image, and if I give a positive interview right before the race, plenty of people will see it. A convincing performance could squash the rumors about a team meltdown."

Roni blew out a breath. "Then I guess Lovejoy is losing confidence in Tucker's charm. Tucker bragged to me that he could settle those folks right down during the meet-and-greet, which should be in full swing by now."

"I hope to hell he can charm them. Maybe he'll

take care of the problem and my interview will be overkill, but I have to do it, regardless."

"I know you do. It's just that you promised Tucker you'd call a meeting with the crew. I hope you're not too crunched for time."

"I'll make sure I'm not." His blue eyes, which had sparkled with happiness a moment ago, became the color of storm clouds. "I purely hate airing dirty laundry."

"I know that, too." She gazed up at him and summoned the temptress who had so recently emerged, the woman who wore tight jeans and low-cut blouses. She lowered her voice. "I'll make it up to you later tonight."

He sucked in a breath. "And *that* makes the whole stupid mess worthwhile." Flashing a quick smile, he tilted his head in the direction of the No. 414 car. "Come on, madam car chief. We have a race to run."

ONLY YEARS OF TRAINING kept Judd focused on the job at hand as he shepherded the car through the last inspection of the day, wolfed down lunch and headed for the drivers' meeting, which was compulsory for the crew chief, too. Until the meeting, Roni had never been far from his sight, which had made concentration even trickier.

Memories of her kiss, her touch and her warm welcome in bed hovered in the background, ready to take over his thoughts if he let down his guard for even a second. God, she was hot, and when she'd promised to make everything better tonight…he'd come close to dragging her to some secluded place where he could ravage that saucy mouth.

Only a complete lack of seclusion had stopped him. Thousands of fans combined with the media and the race teams created the exact opposite of seclusion. He and Roni were in the middle of a three-ring circus. No, make that a ten-ring circus.

As often was the case, the drivers' meeting had been set up with rows of folding chairs in an empty garage bay. Fans crowded around outside the roped-off section, hoping for a glimpse of their favorite driver. As Judd approached, he saw Tucker arrive ahead of him and scribble some autographs on his way into the meeting.

Judd took note of where Tucker was sitting so he could head in that direction. Then he was surrounded by his own fan club. He felt uncomfortable with the whole idea of attracting fans, but somehow he had, and he wasn't the type to ignore them. He gave as many autographs as he dared take time for, but he couldn't be late. The No. 414 car had enough problems without being penalized for the crew chief's tardiness at the meeting.

Going in with a couple of minutes to spare, Judd edged past some guys so he could take the chair on Tucker's left. Tucker didn't acknowledge his presence, but Judd wasn't going to let that stop him from being friendly. He turned toward him. "How did the sponsor thing go?"

Tucker looked at him, then looked away again. "Okay."

If Judd had to guess, he'd say the meet-and-greet had not been all Tucker might have wanted.

"But I've been thinking." Tucker spared Judd another quick glance. "I'd like you to contact the sponsor and tell them the same thing you're going to tell the crew today."

"I take it they weren't particularly welcoming."

Tucker stared straight ahead. "Not so much."

"All right. I'll contact the sponsor." Judd had considered mentioning his upcoming interview but thought better of it. Tucker would probably ask him to work in an apology there, too, so it would go out on national TV. Judd was sure as hell not doing that. He had his limits.

The meeting started on the dot and Judd hoped it wouldn't take long. He had to cram the interview and his little talk with the crew into the remaining time before the start of the race, and the minutes were ticking by.

Apparently luck wasn't on his side, because the meeting ran long. Judd and Tucker started back toward the bay where the team was giving the No. 414 car a last-minute check. Judd had just enough time to make his speech to them, assuming the TV crew didn't show up.

But then he spotted Stan Baker coming his way with a cameraman. Dammit.

Tucker smiled as they approached. "Guess I could squeeze in one more interview."

"Tucker, I'm not sure that they—"

"Hey, relax, Timmons. I'll join the crew in plenty of time for your apology." Tucker made a beeline for Stan. "Hey, how's it going?"

Stan, who'd been covering NASCAR for years, smiled back. "Great. Good luck out there today, Merritt."

"Thanks. Listen, if you have any questions, I have a couple of minutes to spare."

"Actually, we're scheduled to interview your crew chief."

"Is that so?" Tucker turned slowly back to Judd, his gaze calculating. "What're you planning to say, Timmons?"

"That you're a talented driver with an excellent chance to win this thing."

"That's it?" Tucker's implication was clear. "Because this would be a good opportunity to—"

"I don't think so."

Tucker scowled. "Then this interview better be short and sweet, because you're running out of time." Then he shouldered his way through the crowd toward the No. 414 car.

Judd checked his BlackBerry and discovered Tucker was right. Time was of the essence. "I hope this won't take long," he said to Stan. "I really do have to get back to my crew."

"We'll make it as quick as possible." Stan signaled to his cameraman, who hoisted the minicam to his shoulder and aimed the lens at Judd.

"I appreciate that." Judd cleared his throat and vowed to make only positive comments.

Stan adjusted his earbud while he waited for the cameraman's countdown. Then he raised the mike. "We're here with Judd Timmons, crew chief for the Goddess Chocolates team. How do you rate your chances today with Tucker Merritt in the No. 414 car, Judd?" He pointed the mike at Judd.

Judd pumped enthusiasm into his voice. "Great, Stan. Tucker's a terrific driver and the No. 414 car is ready to race. Speaking of that, if you'll excuse me, I need to—"

"We just saw Tucker a moment ago and he didn't look happy. Rumors are flying that there's a problem between you and your driver, something to do with a woman. Can you shed some light on the situation?"

Judd had a split second to decide how to answer, but he was used to dealing in split seconds. In that small window of opportunity, he thought of what Roni would advise him to do. And she would be right.

CHAPTER NINE

RONI HAD BEEN WATCHING the clock, and when Tucker arrived ahead of Judd, she knew they had trouble. "Where's Judd?"

"Interview." Tucker walked away from her and asked Derek how the engine sounded this morning.

Roni groaned. Unless it was the shortest interview in history, Judd wouldn't have time to talk to the crew about Tucker and Loretta. He'd have to go back on his word.

He was too principled to do that, but she wondered how he'd solve the problem. Suddenly it seemed critical for her to see that interview. The logical place was in the lounge of the hauler.

She put a hand on Derek's shoulder. "I'll be right back." Moving as quickly as possible through the crowded garage, she ran out the door and through the infield. There was a big-screen TV in the hauler's lounge. At this point in the day, it would be on.

She made it through the side door of the hauler in record time, and sure enough, the TV was on and

Judd's face filled the screen. She caught the tail end of a sentence.

"...to correct an injustice," he said. "At the end of last season, I was told Tucker Merritt had gone behind my back with a woman I was dating. That information was dead wrong. Tucker has always been loyal to me and the team. I owe him an apology for thinking otherwise. And now, if you'll excuse me, I have a race to run."

Roni was stunned. Judd had sacrificed his pride for the sake of the team. And also for Tucker, who probably had no idea what Judd had just done.

Bolting out the door, she clambered down the steps. Now that Judd had come through with a grand gesture, Tucker needed to know that before he climbed into the No. 414 car.

But she was too late. By the time she made it back, the car was out of the garage and the crew was lining up for the national anthem. She barely made it into her assigned spot in the lineup before the opening bars.

Maybe Judd had found a moment to say something to Tucker, although she doubted it. He'd have been pushed to get back in time, himself. The seasoned crew had handled everything just fine without them, but Roni didn't like a rushed beginning to a race.

Even so, excitement surged through her knowing that this time she'd be able to watch from the war wagon, an elevated box seat designed to give the crew chief and select others a better view of the race.

Lovejoy always watched the first race of the season from there, and he was seated next to Judd when she climbed up. He glanced at her and smiled. "Congratulations on your promotion to car chief."

"Thanks." She put on her headset and looked over at Judd. He was on his headset mike, talking to Dave Ingersoll, the team spotter who was positioned at the top of the grandstand where he could see the entire track.

As the pace car led the field of forty-three cars around the speedway, Judd exchanged some terse words with Tucker. Roni put on her headset, and as she listened to Tucker's response, she knew for certain that he hadn't heard anything about the interview. He was more belligerent than ever.

As the green flag dropped and the cars surged forward, Roni crossed her fingers and hoped that the importance of this race would override Tucker's anger. At first, it seemed as if it might.

But then she realized Judd hadn't been saying much of anything to him. All the instructions had come from the spotter, Dave. He was the only other team member with a mike. But sooner or later, Judd would have to communicate with his driver.

That moment came when Tucker became too impatient with Dave's advice and passed the No. 426 car high in the turn. He made it, but he grazed the wall.

"Easy does it, Tucker," Judd said. "We can't win if we don't finish."

"The car's too tight." Tucker sounded petulant. "I've said that all week."

"We'll fix that when we pit." Judd's tone remained neutral.

"Now that's scary," Tucker said. "All I need is a long pit stop while you jack around with the suspension and I'm totally screwed."

Roni glanced over at Judd.

A muscle bunched in his jaw, but his voice remained calm. "With Roni around, you don't have to worry about that. In the meantime, stay off the high side so you're away from the wall."

"I like the high side."

Judd blew out a breath. "Go low, Tucker, at least until we pit."

Tucker ignored him.

Lovejoy mumbled a swearword and whipped off his headset. Then he leaned toward Judd. "Does Merritt know about that interview you gave?"

Judd shook his head.

"Then tell him."

Judd covered his mike. "He won't believe me."

Lovejoy held out his hand. "Then give that to me. I'll tell him."

Judd lifted off the headset and passed it over to Lovejoy as Roni watched, fascinated. Lovejoy liked being involved in the race, but he'd never talked to one of his drivers in the middle of one.

Lovejoy put on the headset and adjusted the mike. "Tucker, this is Jake."

In the shocked silence that followed, Roni could imagine Tucker doing a mental double take. "Yes, sir, Mr. Lovejoy."

"Apparently you didn't hear about the interview Judd gave prior to the race."

"It didn't concern me."

"As a matter of fact, it did. Judd informed the fans that you're a loyal member of the team and that the rumors about you are based on a lie."

"He *did?* On national TV?"

Roni pressed her lips together to keep from laughing at the disbelief in Tucker's voice.

But he must have realized he'd just questioned the word of his boss, the man who held the purse strings, because he cleared his throat and corrected his response. "I mean, that's great, Mr. Lovejoy. Thanks for letting me know."

"You're welcome. Good luck out there. Now here's your crew chief." Lovejoy handed the headset back to Judd.

And just like that, it became a different race for the No. 414 car. There were still close calls, still hairy moments when Roni wondered if Tucker would wreck, but he didn't. He and Judd worked as a team the way they had before Loretta had ruined their friendship. Although Tucker didn't win, he finished a very decent seventh.

When he returned to the pit and climbed from the car, he was welcomed with cheers and slaps on the back. Roni stood slightly apart so she could enjoy the moment when Judd walked forward, hand outstretched. Tucker grabbed his hand and pulled him into an embrace. The team was whole again.

Then Judd turned and scanned the group. "Where's Roni?"

She found herself being pushed forward by members of the crew until she stood in front of Judd. To her amazement, he put an arm around her shoulder and turned her to face the crew.

"I introduced Roni as our new car chief yesterday," he said. "She's professionally valuable to our team and was a huge factor in our success with this race." He hugged her closer. "She's also personally valuable to me."

Roni's heart rate shot up and her skin flushed. Surely the Iceman wasn't going to publicly declare his affections?

Judd's arm remained firmly around her shoulder as he gazed down at her. "Roni, I hoped to have something to present to you at this point, but it seems to have been delayed, so I—"

"I'm here, I'm here!" Steve, one of the representatives for Goddess Chocolates, held aloft a gigantic gold box of chocolates.

Crew members passed the box forward, with everyone suggesting that the box could be shared.

"Nope," Judd took the box and handed it to her. "These are for the woman I love."

Roni stared at him. Surely she'd misunderstood. Judd couldn't possibly have used the L word. And in public, at that. "Really?"

His voice softened. "Yeah, really." His blue eyes held hers. "Roni, will you be my valentine?"

She would swear someone had just poured a magnum of champagne over her head. The world seemed fizzy and sweet. "Yes."

"So kiss her, Iceman," Tucker said. "Let's do this right."

Roni gazed up at Judd. "You don't have to," she murmured.

"But I want to." He glanced at the huge box of chocolates she held. "Could you get rid of those?"

"But they're your grand gesture."

"You think I'm only capable of one?" He took the chocolates and passed them over to Tucker. Then he pulled her into his arms. "I love you, Roni."

The champagne she'd imagined pouring over her head now seemed to dance through her veins. She hadn't been this happy since…ever. "I love you right back, Judd."

The crew began to chant *kiss her, kiss her, kiss her.*

With a soft smile, he lowered his mouth to hers. For a brief moment she thought about the craziness of it—kissing in the midst of the usual after-race pandemonium with the entire crew looking on. And then it didn't seem crazy at all. It seemed exactly, perfectly, wonderfully right. After all, it was Valentine's Day.

* * * * *

This one's for Karen and Rick.
You make me laugh and you keep me fit.
What a combination!

AN OUTSIDE CHANCE
Nancy Warren

Dear Reader,

Who doesn't love Valentine's Day? The flowers, the chocolate, the hearts everywhere. And the opening of NASCAR season!

For some reason, a lot of my friends have been telling me funny stories lately about online dating disasters, a lot of them having to do with people turning up and being totally different from the person (and photo) they appeared to be online. Why do men (and probably women) present themselves online as someone totally unlike themselves? Do they not realize that if all goes well and they go out for a date it will be pretty obvious they were faking?

I thought this would be a fun place to start a romance, with a woman falling online for a guy who turned out to be a big disaster in person.

In romance, as in life, it's all about this question: And then what happens?

I'm delighted to be sharing these pages with two wonderful women, and terrific writers, Vicki and Dorien.

Happy reading,

Nancy

CHAPTER ONE

WHO HAD THEIR LIFE ruined by a book? Lucy Vander-wal raged as she stomped across the hard-packed sand on Daytona Beach on that fateful day in February.

A book, for goodness' sake. It wasn't like she was somebody famous and her personal trainer, cook, ex-boyfriend or close relative had written an excruciating tell-all memoir revealing what a terrible person she was, while making themselves rich in the process. She was a nobody. A behind the scenes fashion-show dresser from New Jersey.

The book wasn't even about her. Nevertheless, it had ruined her life.

She wouldn't be here were it not for two hundred and eighty-five pages of advice she never should have taken. In fact, if she were truly honest, she'd have to say it was Auntie Grace who had ruined her life by giving her the book in the first place.

On her thirtieth birthday, Auntie Grace, who was as kind as she was tactless, presented the carefully wrapped gift at the party her family had thrown for her in an Italian restaurant. Her Auntie Grace was a frugal woman and this was not the first time the wrapping had been used. The wrap pictured sparkly princesses on a pink background. The paper showed several folds that her aunt had tried to iron out and Lucy could see the faded spot where she'd carefully removed the tape.

Last Chance for Love, the book was titled. In smaller print came the subtitle, *Advice for the Over 30 Single Woman.*

Most of her family had laughed when she showed them her gift, but there were a few sympathetic glances her way. Since Lucy was well brought up and an expert on not hurting people's feelings, she'd taken the gift with good grace, lugged it home along with the rest of her presents and shelved it among her cookbooks. Naturally, she couldn't throw the thing away in case Auntie Grace came over to her apartment, in which case she'd have to display the book prominently on her coffee table among the clutter of current fashion magazines.

Only a desperate woman would read a book like that, and Lucy wasn't desperate, not then.

That was two years ago. Now, at thirty-two, she suddenly felt as if her biological clock had turned into a gong. *Gong, gong, gong.* The sound echoed through her at the oddest times, as though her chance to grab what she wanted out of life was going, going, gone. She wanted a husband, a home and kids. But even she could see that in an industry where a straight male was rarer than the spotted owl, and living in New York City, where a long-term relationship was anything that lasted more than two weekends, she wasn't getting closer to her hoped-for future.

She didn't even love her job as much as she once had. Dressing high-strung supermodels was all about speed, tact, dishing out free therapy and taking abuse. A lot of abuse. She understood models were under enormous pressure, she really did. Being 6'1" and trying to survive on a thousand calories a day without ever aging would stress anybody out.

The day was sunny and surprisingly warm for February, though of course she was in Florida, having left the cold and gray of New York behind her. Normally, the sunshine and splashing waves would have filled her with happiness, but now they only reminded her of what a fool she'd been.

Over a man.

A man she'd met by following the advice in that stupid book.

Chapter One: Go Where the Men Are.

Well, that had worked out well.

Almost without volition, her arms started to windmill as she considered how Dan Krankill had made a fool out of her.

"I hate you, Dan Krankill!" she shouted to the winds, and the lone pelican drifting past.

The flailing felt pretty good, so she kept at it, not caring a bit that she must look like a crazy person. Who knew her in Florida except for Dan Krankill, liar, cheat and attempted seducer of desperate thirty-two-year-olds?

Maybe rage therapy would be more appropriate in a therapist's office, but acting out her anger on the beach was definitely working.

She filled her lungs with air and imagined the creep she'd all but fallen in love with online standing in front of her. "You are a liar, a cheat," she yelled to the imaginary Dan. "Way uglier in person than your profile picture." She worked herself up to the worst part. "Oh, yeah. And married!"

At the last word her rage found its zenith and her fists bunched tighter than Rocky's as she imagined taking Dan Krankill down. With a cry of fury, she let him have it. Her head filled with comic book type sounds as she punched her fists into the air: *Bam, Whack, Boom.*

Kazaam!

So real was her fantasy that she felt as though her fist connected with solid flesh and muscle. Then she heard a grunt of pain so real that she opened her eyes, horrified to discover that she had somehow sucker punched a jogger.

As the young man hit the ground, she saw the earbuds of his iPod pop out of his ears and hit the sand. His ball cap had sailed from his head, his dark glasses skewed to one side, and his knees came up as he gasped for breath.

She was conscious of pain radiating up her arm and into her shoulder, and realized she had packed years of frustration into that punch, never dreaming she'd hit anything but air.

"Oh, my gosh," Lucy cried, falling to her knees beside the poor guy. "Are you all right?"

Gray eyes blinked at her, at least the parts she could see from behind the crooked glasses. They were regarding her very warily, as though the man on the ground was unsure how to handle her.

"I'm so sorry. I'm not really a crazy person. I was acting out my anger. I had no idea there was anyone in the vicinity."

"I was looking at the ground," he panted. "Didn't see you."

"Didn't you hear me?"

He pointed to his iPod. "I heard Springsteen."

He struggled to sitting, pulled off the glasses and looked at her fully. "You practicing for the middle-weight championship?"

"No. Just enjoying a man-hating rant."

His eyes narrowed and scanned her body as though checking for weapons. He must have seen that her short floral skirt and green tank top weren't hiding anything. Still, she made haste to reassure him.

"Not all men. One man. Dan Krankill." She thought she might have chipped a tooth getting the name out.

"What did he do?" the young man asked her. She thought maybe he needed a minute to get his breath back and the kindest thing she could do was to keep talking until he was able to stand.

"He lied to me, got me to Florida under false pretenses, wasn't at all what he seemed like on line, and I think he's married." She scowled. "And here I am with a week booked in a condo, tickets to Sunday's race and no romantic Valentine story."

"So you tried to punch out Daytona?" He crinkled his eyes against the sun and gave her a half grin.

And in that moment she realized how cute he was. He had dark, short-trimmed hair, twinkling gray eyes that seemed to regard the world with humor, sharp cheekbones in a tanned face and a nose that had been broken at least once.

His build was athletic. Ripped even, she thought, noting the defined arm muscles and the athletic, runner's legs beneath his shorts. Now that she thought about it, punching him had been like slugging a cinder-block wall. Her arm still hurt.

He even looked oddly familiar, which was ridiculous since she didn't know a soul in Daytona. Unless…

"You don't spend a lot of time on line, do you?"

"Not much."

"Do you ever hang out at NASCARfan.com?"

The twinkle was more pronounced. "Once in a while."

"Hmm. Maybe I've seen you there. Or maybe I really am losing my mind. You seem kind of familiar." The sun was beating down on them and she was worried that her 30 SPF wasn't up to the job. "Are you well enough to stand?"

"Yeah. Of course." He rose in one smooth motion, holding his hand down to help her up. She couldn't believe he was being nice to her after she had knocked him over.

But she had and she didn't want to think of him hurt because of her. "Should I take you to a doctor?"

"What for?"

"In case you have...I don't know, internal injuries or something."

He laughed as though he'd tried to stop the sound and couldn't. "No offense, but you punch like a girl."

"I knocked you flat," she reminded him. She was relieved she hadn't hurt him badly, but still. She had her pride. She worked out regularly. Could do twenty-five full pushups at a time. She was no weakling.

"You caught me right in the solar plexus," he explained, rubbing his upper belly. "Knocked the wind out of me is all. I'll be fine."

"Okay." She stood there, realizing she didn't want him to go. He was the only person she knew to talk to in Florida, and he was exactly the kind of man Dan Krankill's fake profile had led her to expect. "If only Dan Krankill had turned out to be you."

He laughed. Which made her slap her hand over her mouth. "Did I say that out loud?"

"Yeah. You did." He stood considering her for a moment; she thought he looked a little sorry for her, which made two of them. "Tell you what. I don't want you taking me to any doctor, but you can buy me a cold drink."

It was a pity gesture, she knew that, of course, but right now she was willing to grasp at the offered lifeline. "Thanks," she said. "I passed a diner up that way."

CHAPTER TWO

WHAT WAS HE DOING? Sawyer Patton asked himself
as he and his assailant walked side by side up to the
diner. He replaced his ball cap and dark glasses and
stuffed his music player in his pocket. He didn't
think anyone would recognize him, but he kept his
head down anyway, hoping there weren't any more
practitioners of beach rage therapy planted in his
path. If there were, he relied on his companion to
steer him around them.

Not that Sawyer was the most famous driver in
NASCAR. In fact, since this was his first NASCAR
Sprint Cup Series race ever, he was about the least
famous, but his picture seemed to him to be everywhere in town and he wasn't yet all that assured
around fans.

After flattening him during a violent emotional
outburst, the woman beside him hadn't seemed all that
crazy; she had a kind of naive goofiness about her that
reminded him of his sister, Emily. He suspected that's
why he'd chosen to spend more time with her when
his handlers probably had other things for him to do.

But, in the twenty minutes or so since she'd knocked him down, he hadn't even thought about the upcoming race, which was a twenty-minute break he badly needed. He could think of nothing but the fact that he was about to make his debut at Daytona's big race no matter how hard he tried.

He knew he was ready. He was part of a team that had a history of picking winners. This was the fulfillment of a dream he'd held since he was eight years old. He even thought he'd be fine once the flag fell and the race was on, but the days leading up to the race were tough. Excitement, anticipation, determination to do well and the constantly fought battle with fear of failure were messing with his mind. Talking to a woman who had more problems than he did, especially one who reminded him of home, was irresistible. Besides, he felt sorry for her. She seemed like a nice woman in a tough spot.

Maybe they could help each other out.

She stopped, before they reached the diner, putting a hand on his arm and turning to face him. "I'm Lucy, by the way."

She held out her hand. There was a musical tinkle and flash as the bangles on her wrist danced. She had nice, slim arms. Good shoulders. He bet she worked out. Recalled the punch and was sure of it.

You'd never confuse her with a centerfold, but he saw enough of those pumped up bodies at home in California. This woman obviously didn't have implants, no spray tan darkened her fair skin, her short, curly brown hair was free of extensions. Even her teeth weren't orthodontically perfected. Her front teeth overlapped slightly, which struck him as being like her. Slightly off center, but in a good way.

A pair of frank brown eyes were her best feature and over these her brows were raised in a silent question.

"I'm Sawyer," he said. He'd known the second he suggested a drink that she'd soon find out who he was. Maybe she didn't spend as much time on NASCARfan.com as she thought she did, for her forehead scrunched for a second, as though she was close to placing him but couldn't quite do it. "Sawyer Patton."

Now her eyes opened wide. "The brand-new driver?"

"Not a brand-new driver. New to the Sprint Cup series, that's all."

"How exciting."

"Dream of a lifetime," he answered, pleased to note that she took his profession in stride.

The diner wasn't very busy at eleven in the morning and they found themselves in a quiet corner booth. The place looked like a set from the old sitcom, *Happy Days,* right down to the red jukebox.

"Ooh," Lucy cried, perusing the menu, "real old-fashioned milkshakes. Made with ice cream. That's what I'm having!"

He nearly gaped at her. He couldn't remember the last time he'd been out with a woman who would order a milkshake.

The waitress came over to them with her pad. "Two milkshakes," he said. He glanced enquiringly at Lucy, sitting across from him and looking as excited about her milkshake as a little kid. "Chocolate?"

"Of course."

He nodded. "Two chocolate shakes."

"Coming right up."

He shifted on the vinyl seat of the booth and as he did so he was aware of the slight ache below his ribs where Miss Lucy had socked him one. The memory brought back the extraordinary bits of information she'd let fall and—maybe because of that fleeting resemblance to his sister, Emily or maybe simply because he couldn't think of anything else to say, he leaned forward and said, "Okay, I need to know why a woman like you would come all the way to Florida to meet a guy she found on the Internet."

She straightened her paper placemat on the table-top until it exactly lined up with the chrome border. Then she looked up at him. "Haven't you ever seen the movie *You've Got Mail*?"

"Yep. So have a lot of predators, I bet. Creeps and perverts troll the Internet looking for victims. You know that." He couldn't believe he was talking to her the way he'd talk to Emily, but she didn't seem offended. Maybe she had an older brother. But if so, what was the guy thinking letting her go on this crazy stunt?

Now she straightened the stainless steel utensils and made a show of placing the paper napkin on her lap. "It was NASCARfan.com. He seemed like a really nice guy. The kind I never meet." She stopped fiddling with the cutlery and looked at him straight on. "It's all the fault of that stupid book."

He was getting confused. "What stupid book?"

"This book my aunt got me for my birthday. *Last Chance for Love. Advice to the Woman Over 30.*"

He was surprised she was more than thirty. He'd have guessed she was younger than him, but in fact she was a few years older. "This book told you to hook up with some dude on line?"

"Not exactly. *Go Where the Men Are.* That's the title of chapter one."

"Are you kidding me?"

A dimple appeared in her cheeks when she smiled. "No. It's the most ridiculous book. I can't believe I even read it, but I did and since I work in the fashion industry, which, believe me, is not where the men are, I started looking for new interests. Like stock car racing."

Their milkshakes came and for a minute neither of them said a word, simply sucked the thick, luscious, icy-cold drinks.

"Oh, that is good," she said at last. "I haven't had a chocolate shake in years."

Her simple enjoyment was almost childlike. Whoever took the time to really taste food and drink? He thought that the crazier and more exciting his life got, the more he had to remember to stop and smell the roses. Or taste the milkshakes.

"Did you just tell me you got interested in NASCAR to meet men?"

"Sure. Initially. I liked it better than other sports. The people in the online forums were really friendly, too. Which is how I started hanging out in the chat rooms. One thing led to another and Dan and I started chatting and e-mailing privately. It was like a luscious secret. We were talking every day, sometimes several times. He was funny and smart, and after a few months we decided to meet." She scowled. "Daytona was his idea. Because the big race is so close to Valentine's Day. It seemed so romantic that I said 'yes.'" Her elbow was resting on the table and she opened her palm and smacked her forehead into her hand. "How could I have been so stupid?"

He was wondering that himself.

"I took a vacation, booked a condo and decided to take the plunge."

"Does he know where you're staying?" he asked in a conversational tone.

She glanced up, her big brown eyes darkening. "No. I'm not that stupid. We agreed to meet at the track. It seemed appropriate."

"What happened when you met him?" He wished

he could have witnessed the meet-up. It must have been something to leave her ranting mad.

Another couple came in and were seated at the booth across from them. He huddled lower in his seat and Lucy dropped her voice. "First, I didn't recognize him. He hardly looks anything like the profile picture he posted on NASCARfan.com. He'd either stolen a picture of a way hotter guy to use, or it was him from ten years and fifty pounds ago. Back when he had hair." She sucked more milkshake. "Not that I cared that much what he looked like, but it made me wonder what else he'd fudged, you know?"

Sawyer nodded, fascinated.

"We talked for a few minutes, but he didn't even seem like the same guy I'd been e-mailing with. He wasn't funny and he sure didn't seem very bright. I thought maybe he was just nervous or something."

"People don't normally change their whole personality when they're nervous."

She nodded. "You're right. Then he's carrying a duffel. Says he left it so late to book a room that nothing was available. Is there a couch or something in my condo he could crash on? Well, that was the first time he'd mentioned having nowhere to stay." She glanced up at him and he watched her cheeks pinken. "Of course I was hoping this week would be a whirlwind romance, but I wasn't going to move in with the guy the first day I meet him."

"He's got a nerve."

"Hah, it gets better." She was really warming up to her theme now and had forgotten to lower her voice. "I'm standing there, trying to figure out how to tactfully tell him he can't stay at my place when his cell phone rings. He tells me it's a client, but something about the way he was talking didn't sound like business. He held the phone up to his ear with his left hand and when the sunlight hit his fingers I could see the whiter line where his wedding ring belonged. Not only was it paler, but the skin on his ring finger was dented like he took off his ring ten minutes before I got there."

"Oh, that is tacky."

"You think?"

"What did you do then?" Since she'd mown him down on the aftermath of her encounter, he figured the actual confrontation had to be pretty good.

"I waited until he got off the phone and then I asked him if he had any kids. And he looked at me all funny. Because of course we'd talked on line and he'd told me he wasn't married and was hoping to settle down in the next couple of years and have kids. He started to sputter something and I interrupted him and told him I didn't date married men."

"Good for you."

"He put on this big offended act—how could I not trust him after all we'd been to each other, you know the routine—but he was so dumb he'd forgotten to take his family photo off the screen of his cell phone.

As he was claiming to be single and waving his hands around, his wife and kids were swinging back and forth in front of my face."

Sawyer started to laugh. He couldn't help it.

After a stunned moment, she joined in. "I never, ever thought I would find that funny." She looked up at him, her eyes dancing. "You know what his last words to me were?"

"I'm sorry?" he guessed.

She shook her head, grinning. "His last words were, 'Now where am I going to stay?'" She laughed in a way that used her whole body, and was infectious as hell. He laughed along with her.

"How about you? Since your vacation got off to a rocky start, are you staying?"

"Heck, yes. I might have become a fan for slightly unorthodox reasons, but I love racing. This is my first live race, too. I'm pumped."

What was it about her? As soon as she started telling him her crazy stories, and getting so excited about a milkshake, he found himself savoring every drop of his own. Somehow, the fact that the day he both longed for and dreaded was fast approaching had all but escaped his mind.

Lucy was the best anti-anxiety med around.

He waited until the slurping sounds of her sucking up the last of her drink were done and she'd licked her lips for the last time.

He said, "I have an idea."

CHAPTER THREE

LUCY'S REALLY BAD DAY had amazingly taken a huge turn for the better. She couldn't believe she was sitting here, drinking milkshakes with a hot young driver. He didn't seem to be in a big hurry to leave, either, which was nice.

She liked his frank gaze, and that slightly boyish uncertainty about him.

"What's your idea?" she asked.

"I have to get back to the track, but I was wondering if you'd like to come with me and hang out for a bit?"

Her heart sank a little. Of course he had to get back to the track. He enjoyed a wildly busy, celebrity athlete's life and he was still kind enough to take pity on poor, duped Lucy.

She put on a brave smile and shook her head. "That's okay. You must have a million things to do. I'll grab a book and sit out by the pool or something."

"Lucy, I'm not asking you because I feel sorry for you. I really want you to come hang out."

"Really?"

"Yes."

"Why?"

He laughed. "I don't know. Because you're cute and kind of funny." His eyes grew serious for a moment. "And..." He dropped the serious expression, sat back and crossed his arms on his impressive chest. "Wait a minute, I'm a driver, I'm not supposed to have to talk women into hanging out with me. Didn't NASCARfan.com teach you anything?"

She bit her lip, wishing she were the kind of woman hot athletes went for. But she was a thirty-two-year-old spinster who couldn't even get online dating right. "I don't want to distract you."

His gaze grew intense and as it connected with hers, she thought, aha! He did want her to distract him. Of course. She'd been through this same stage fright with any number of models. She nearly always got the brand-new ones because Lucy was known for her ability to calm performance anxiety. Maybe somebody preparing to walk a runway in six-inch heels under the scrutiny of the world's fashionistas, and a guy preparing to drive a car at a hundred and eighty miles an hour around a track under the scrutiny of tens of thousands of NASCAR fans had more in common than she'd have imagined.

Well, he'd been so amazingly nice to her considering how they met that she figured the least she could do was try to help him relax for a bit.

"You won't distract me," he said in a tone that

confirmed her assessment that distraction was exactly what he wanted from her.

"Okay, then. Thanks. I'd love to come and hang out for a bit." She was struck by an idea. "Do you think I could have my picture taken with you?"

"Now you're acting like a proper fan."

She giggled. "It's not really for me."

"Oh? Who's it for?"

She sat back in the booth, knowing that what she was thinking of doing made her a mean-spirited, re-vengeful woman. "I want to post it on NASCAR-fan.com. Where Dan Krankill will see it." She glanced up, eyes full of mischief. "If you could act like we're pretty close, that would be even better."

"Remind me never to piss you off," he said, laughing with her once again.

The bill came, and in spite of his arguments, she insisted on paying for the milkshakes.

As they left the diner, she thought there was something she should probably find out, sooner rather than later. "Not that it's any of my business, but do you have a girlfriend?"

"Nope. No wife, no girlfriend." He turned his head to face her and said, "And I can prove it."

He dug into his pocket and pulled out his cell phone. When he opened the screen, there was a pic-ture of a black Labrador puppy where Dan Krankill's phone had sported a family photo.

"Oh, how darling. Yours?"

"Yep. He lives with my folks when I'm on the road, but he's mine."

She thought that a man who carried around a photo of his dog and who could willingly spend the day with a woman who had punched him out—even if it had been an accident—was a man she definitely wanted to know better.

She asked the obvious next question.

"What should I wear to the track?"

"You look fine for the track," he assured her. But it seemed to her that most people wore jeans or shorts to the track, and shirts and gear with their favorite drivers plastered all over them. They wore sneakers or work boots. Not funky little sandals with jeweled flowers that showed off her pedicure. In a spirit of romantic excitement, she'd had her toes painted a color called Passionate Pomegranate. After her experience with Dan she should have them repainted in Moronic Mauve.

In fact, the shoes were the only thing he commented on. "Probably can't take you in the garage without close-toed shoes on, but maybe Sam can lend you some sneakers or something."

"Sam?"

"My personal assistant." His lightning swift grin lit up his face. "And I am still not used to having a personal assistant, or a manager, or a team or sponsors." He took a deep breath. "Sometimes it kind of freaks me out, you know?"

She nodded. "You're under a lot of pressure to perform."

"Yeah. And it's not only me, now. People depend on me for their paycheck."

What he needed was diversion. To think about something else for a while. If he was a stressed out model she'd ask about the latest boyfriend, the cheating ex, or whatever man was currently top of mind. Figuring the same logic would apply to a nervous driver she said, "Tell me about your dog."

"He's a great dog. A black Lab. Tons of energy. He can chase a ball all day and still want to go for a swim at night. And he's smart. We have this game where I hide all his toys and he goes around and finds them all."

She hadn't had a dog since she was a kid and she loved hearing about this one. "What's his name?"

Sawyer's face screwed up as though this was a painful subject. "What difference does it make?"

"I don't know. I can't keep referring to him as 'your dog.'"

"Bonanza. His name's Bonanza."

"I see. Um, you were a fan of the old Western show?"

"I didn't name him." He sighed. "Bonanza's a rescue dog. I saw his picture in the paper and felt like I had to have him, you know?"

She remembered seeing the pictures of the fake Dan Krankill on the Net and feeling the same way.

She guessed that Sawyer Patton's instincts were more reliable.

"So I went to see him. He was still young, maybe eight months old. We took to each other right away and I figured I could train him to answer to another name. But I told you he was smart. He's also stubborn. He had a name and he was sticking with it. Even if it's the most retarded name a dog ever got stuck with. He doesn't care. Won't even contemplate answering to anything else. Probably amuses him to hear me yelling 'Bonanza!' like a damn fool."

She could picture Sawyer, out with his dog, playing ball or running in a park and the image struck her as adorable. "I would love to meet Bonanza."

"You'll probably get to. My parents are coming out to watch me in my first big race. I begged them not to but they insisted. They're driving their camper across the country. Should be here in a day or two."

"It will be nice to have your parents here," she said soothingly. "They're your biggest fans. And they are bringing your dog." And pets, she knew, were very good for calming the nerves.

He snorted. "Not only my parents. They're dragging both of my sisters along with them."

"You have two sisters?"

"Yep. Emily and Roberta."

By this time they'd arrived at a gray pickup truck. He pulled out keys. "Are you parked around here?"

"I walked down from my condo. My rental's parked there."

"Hop in. I'll drive you to the track."

"I could go grab my own vehicle."

He shook his head. "It's easier this way. When you get tired, I'll run you back home."

"I don't want to impose."

He shot her a look he no doubt gave his sisters when they were acting like girls. "Hop in."

She did. "Am I correct in assuming you don't have any brothers?"

"Yep." As though anticipating her next question, he said, "I'm in the middle. One older sister and one younger."

He pulled out into traffic and after a few minutes she relaxed. He drove like a normal person, clearly keeping his speed-demon tendencies for race days.

The closer they got to the track, the busier everything seemed. The huge campgrounds were filling up and a lot of tailgate parties were already in session. The folks who followed NASCAR quite literally, driving from race to race and setting up camp for the duration, were amazingly well-equipped in their homes away from home.

She saw portable barbecues already smoking, a family putting the final touches on an outdoor dining tent and a small clothesline with wash hanging out to dry.

There were vehicles of all sorts, from fancy motor

homes that probably cost more than her parents' house, to campers that looked as though they'd been around for Woodstock.

Whatever their mode of transport, the fans were here for recreation, to be part of the spectacle, to support their driver. And then they'd pack up and do it all again next Sunday.

When Dan and she had met this morning it had been outside the gates, so it was a thrill to get inside, especially with a driver. They parked the truck and walked straight to the garage area, an ant hill of activity as teams prepared for qualifying.

It was thrilling to be inside. The beautiful grounds, the huge trailers set up to sell everything from shirts and ball caps to drink containers. The fans wandering around.

She was suddenly, inexplicably, an insider.

Maybe Auntie Grace hadn't ruined her life. Maybe she was an unusual kind of fairy godmother.

CHAPTER FOUR

WHEN THEY GOT TO HIS GARAGE, Sawyer put an arm around her shoulders and introduced her to his key people. It was nice to have his arm around her, especially after the emotional humiliation of the morning, but she wasn't fooling herself. This arm was brotherly.

No wonder she was thirty-two and still single. The men she worked with all treated her like their mother and therapist combined into one very efficient package, or she got the Dan Krankill type who pretty clearly was looking for the marriage benefits without commitment, or she met the perfect guy, gorgeous, funny, successful—and he treated her like his sister.

With a sinking feeling in the pit of her stomach, she suspected that a peek at his birth certificate would confirm her as his older sister.

Oh, well, it was a beautiful day, she was having a truly great adventure and there was no point wasting her life wishing for what she couldn't have.

She wondered how he'd introduce her and gave

him marks for class when he didn't mention the part where she beat him up on the beach. Or the part where she'd made a date with a creep she only knew from the Internet. He said, "Hey, guys, this is Lucy, a friend of mine from New York. She's in town for the race so I thought I'd show her around." It was even true, if he considered that after knowing each other only a couple of hours they were already friends.

She very much hoped she was the only one who had noticed the tiny pause after her first name when he realized he didn't know her last.

"This is Stu Cameron, my team manager."

She shook hands with the big, bull-like man wearing a Sawyer Patton ball cap. "Hi," she said, giving him her big, friendly smile. "Lucy Vanderwal." She said it nice and loud so Sawyer could hear.

After that she met the jackman, various mechanics and Sam, his personal assistant, who seemed like a very energetic and organized young woman. She carried a clipboard and Lucy could see there were color-coded blocks on there—his calendar of events, she assumed.

"Where have you been?" Sam cried to Sawyer, the second she'd shaken Lucy's hand.

"Hanging out with Lucy. Why?"

"You didn't answer your cell."

"I guess I didn't hear it. I had the music on when I was running." He looked a little sheepish. "Never thought to check messages."

"You have to check your messages." She glanced at a black sports watch with an oversize dial. "One of the TV networks wants to interview you. The reporter is from L.A. She's doing a feature on the new faces in sports."

"Cool."

"You're not kidding. The multisport approach means you'll reach lots of potential new fans."

"What's the feature called?"

Sam groaned. "I was hoping you wouldn't ask me. Remember, it's great exposure."

"Lots of potential new fans," Stu said, sounding as if he was holding back a grin.

Sawyer folded his arms across his chest and glanced from one to the other. "And it's called?"

Sam bit her lip. "It's called *Sunday Studs*."

"The price of fame, son," Stu said, slapping him on the back in a way that suggested he was never going to live this down.

"We have to get right over to the media center. She's interviewing all three rookie drivers this season." Sam reached behind her. "Here's a clean shirt. Go change in the hauler."

With a groan, he disappeared into the huge hauler that not only housed his race car and every possible spare part, but also had a lounge in the back.

He emerged in less than a minute, tucking the black T-shirt into his jeans.

"Let's go," Sam said, already on the move.

"Wait," Lucy said.

"What?" He and Sam turned to her in unison.

"You can't wear that."

"What's wrong with it?"

She was so used to working in the fashion industry she couldn't believe anyone had to ask. "That shirt's too big. You're a Sunday Stud, not his kid brother. You need a shirt that fits and, frankly, given your fitness level and the nice muscles in your chest, I'd recommend something slightly snug." Sam had her mouth hanging open and Stu looked as if he was going to burst out laughing. She quelled the manager with a glance, smiled at Sam and explained. "I'm a fashion dresser. It's my job to make people look great in clothes. If we're selling Sawyer as a stud, we've got to put together the right package."

"We don't have time."

"Five minutes." Lucy could be bossy when the situation required it, and in her professional opinion, this was an emergency. Sawyer's image would be set this season, and she thought a sexy young guy who had sisters and was nice to strange women was going to be a real asset to the female fans. "You know women account for forty percent of NASCAR fans. Believe me, if they're looking for a Sunday Stud they want to see his best features."

"Lucy…" Sawyer groaned the word.

"She's right," Stu said, giving her an approving nod.

"I need a smaller shirt. Is there one inside?"

Sam nodded, glancing at Sawyer, who shrugged.

"Come on," Lucy said, taking his hand and leading him into the hauler. Once the door banged behind them she said, "I didn't want to mention this in front of Stu but I also need a comb and some hair gel."

"Aw, Lucy, you're not going to make me look like one of those male model types, are you?"

She grinned. "Like a very sexy, studly one."

"I don't have any hair gel."

Sam handed her another T-shirt and without even thinking about it she started to tug off Sawyer's T-shirt as though he were a toddler. He shook his head at her, then held out his arms and helped her get the too-big shirt off him.

The chest he bared was even better than she'd imagined. Tanned, muscular, his belly a perfect six-pack, he had exactly the right amount of chest hair. His arms and shoulders were well-defined and she found herself longing to lay her head on that delicious chest and feel his strong arms enfold her.

Frankly, she thought the studliest thing he could do was turn up shirtless, but she had a strong feeling he'd tell her to mind her own business and stuff himself back into that tent-size T-shirt, so she kept her mouth shut.

She took the smaller shirt and fitted it over his head. "Much better," she said, when she saw the way it clung lovingly to his chest, the way she'd like to.

He made to walk past her but she pushed him gently toward the bathroom.

He resisted. "I already brushed my teeth. And I told you I don't have gel."

She opened her purse. "No problem. I always carry some with me."

"Girl hair gel?" He looked horrified.

"Unisex gel. Don't be a baby."

"Tick-tock," Sam reminded them.

She pushed him into the bathroom, squeezed a little of her gel on her palms and then ran her fingers through his hair. Thick, lush hair that she would love to play in. Working in the small space meant she was all but pressed against him. She could feel the heat coming off his body. Their gazes connected in the mirror and something zinged between them, so her fingers stalled for a moment and she felt as though she'd run out of air.

The door of the hauler slammed and jerked her back to reality. She pushed and pulled a little with her fingertips and where there had been hat head, now there was style.

She nodded, insanely pleased with herself. "Perfect." The dark shirt brought out the silver color in his gray eyes and molded nicely to his body, disappearing into a decent pair of jeans. Thank goodness he was from California, where they understood designer jeans.

"Thanks, Lucy," he said. "Hey, you'd better come along in case I need any touch-ups."

"I'd like that."

She didn't think he really needed her so much as he didn't want to leave her alone, which was nice of him. Plus, it would be fun to see inside the media center.

He dragged her out of the hauler and she found Sam waiting in a golf cart, apparently the approved mode of transport at the track. Sawyer jumped on beside Sam, Lucy jumped on the backseat and they were off.

They flew by rows of haulers and busy teams, then out to where the fans wandered, and she caught glimpses of the track. She already had her ticket for Sunday's race but she had no idea where she'd be sitting.

She knew who she'd be cheering for, though.

CHAPTER FIVE

"I CANNOT BELIEVE they talked me into taking off my shirt," Sawyer complained. Not, he was pretty sure, for the last time. He'd naively believed all a NASCAR driver had to do was drive fast, treat fans nicely and be a good sport.

He'd had no idea partial nudity and features like *Sunday Studs* would be involved.

He was slumped on the couch in his brand-new home-away-from-home luxury motor home, chugging a soft drink while *FOX News* played on the big-screen TV that took up half the living area. Lucy sat beside him, sipping her drink.

Lucy, ever-perky Lucy, only grinned at him, her brown eyes sparkling. He'd never seen such sparkly eyes, as though every sight was a wonder to her. "Sawyer, one day you will be old and have a big potbelly hanging over the sides of your recliner. Think how happy you'll be then to show your grandkids that once upon a time, Grandpappy was a Sunday Stud."

"You're enjoying this way too much."

"You are too sensitive. Women everywhere are going to love that feature. You could end up with sponsors you never dreamed of." Her head tilted and she regarded him with fake innocence. He heard the musical jingle of her bracelets as she raised her hands. "Underwear makers and deodorant manufacturers, for instance. And shaving cream ads often use topless men."

"I swear, I'm going to come over there and—"

But he never got a chance to finish describing some punishment they both knew he'd never dish out. Stu came in, looking keenly at Sawyer, as though his gaze could burrow right down into the pit of his fears, where he couldn't stop worrying that he was going to choke.

Fail spectacularly after he'd come this close to his dream, let everybody down who'd believed in him, from his family to Stu to the guys changing his tires.

"How you doing?" Stu wanted to know.

"Pretty good."

"Ready for qualifying tomorrow?"

"You bet."

The older man nodded his head, probably not fooled for a second. He'd been around racing for years and had to know that Sawyer wasn't feeling exactly relaxed.

"Good. We're making a few adjustments after your last ride. We'll probably be working late. Why don't you head out now and get some rest. And drink plenty of water. You want to be well hydrated for tomorrow."

"I will." Over the course of a race, a stock car's interior heated up like an oven. The qualifying race in Daytona was done in two 150-mile races. There was a complicated procedure to qualify for Sunday's race that involved his team's standings the previous season, his own—in this case nonexistent—record, and his finishing position in lap races and in tomorrow's qualifier.

There wasn't a lot at this point that he could do but he knew Stu was right. If he started the day hydrated, he'd be better prepared. And right now he was willing to do everything he could to improve his chances of making a good showing tomorrow.

"Good. Just remember everything I told you. Don't start out too fast. Take your time, get the feel of the track. You're the new boy out there and everybody knows it, so don't act cocky. Don't act like you're asleep at the wheel, either. You know what I'm saying?"

"Yeah." And the pep talk really wasn't working.

Stu seemed to realize it for he stopped talking. "Okay. Get some rest. See you in the morning."

After he left, Lucy placed her drink neatly on the table and said, "I should probably get going. There must be shuttles or something back to the beach."

"I said I'd drive you home. I will."

Twin furrows formed between her brows. "But shouldn't you rest?"

"It's six o'clock at night. If I try to rest, I'll go

crazy. Come on," he said, and grabbed a hoodie, his dark glasses and a cap. "Let's go get some pizza."

"You don't have to—"

"Really, I feel like pizza and I want to eat it far away from anyone whose livelihood depends on how well I do this week."

She picked up her bag. "Okay, but I should warn you, I like to mix and match strange ingredients on my pizzas."

And just like that she started to amuse him and he forgot about tomorrow. "Like what?"

Her curls tossed as she turned to him. "Have you ever had anchovy and pineapple?"

"I don't believe I have."

"I don't recommend it. Peanuts and chocolate is surprisingly delicious, though. Not with a red sauce, obviously. You have to stick with white."

He chuckled. "I can see we are going to have to order two pizzas. I'm pretty much a pepperoni and mushroom kind of guy."

"And you're from California? At least put some basil and artichoke hearts on there."

"Nope."

Sam drove them in the golf cart back to his truck, where Lucy politely thanked her.

"You're welcome. It was great meeting you. Sawyer, is your cell phone on?"

"Yeah."

"Good."

In the end they agreed on a pizza with the works at a little place downtown that had been recommended to him. He tried to put all of Stu's words of advice out of his mind, except the part about hydrating. He drank a lot of water with his meal.

While they talked, Lucy told him about some of the wilder moments of her life behind the scenes in the fashion world. Having dated a couple of models, he could imagine that her job wasn't the easiest, but she made it sound so comical, and was always willing to make herself the butt of the joke, that he enjoyed her stories enormously.

She made him laugh, she made him forget tomorrow, she made him relax.

Until dinner was over and she made noises about going back to her condo. He suddenly realized he didn't want to be alone. He'd go crazy cooped up in that motor home, watching crap on TV. He needed to get some of the free-flowing adrenaline out of his system.

Once they were outside, he considered the options.

"Hey, do you feel like playing pool?"

"I don't know how."

He could teach her, but he needed something fast-paced to do tonight, and patient instruction wasn't it.

"Run on the beach?"

"Last time we tried that you ended up flat on your

back, sucking wind," she reminded him. With a touch of completely inappropriate pride, he thought. "Besides, we just ate."

He glanced up and down the street as though he'd find inspiration, but he saw more restaurants, a convenience store and a quartet of old people on motorcycles. "I don't know. I need to do something. Do you have any ideas?"

She thought for a second. "Bowling?"

"Bowling?"

"Sure. I like bowling. And it's quite physical, also competitive, which I assume you are."

"But—"

"I should probably warn you that I was on the championship team in junior high. So don't get all upset when you lose."

"That's it." He yanked off the dark glasses and stalked up to her. "You started the day by knocking me on my ass, as you keep reminding me, then you put goop in my hair and, I swear, you positively enjoyed it when I had to take off my damn shirt for the cameras."

"Oh, I did," she murmured, her dark eyes twinkling at him.

"Now you're suggesting you can beat me at bowling? You do realize I'm a trained athlete?"

She put her hands on her hips. "How 'bout you put your money where your big mouth is?" she suggested.

He moved even closer, right into her personal

space. Her eyes widened slightly but she didn't look a bit intimidated. If anything, she looked... What she looked was good enough to kiss. The same strange impulse that had struck him when they were stuck in that tiny bathroom together and she was messing with his hair, her body lightly touching his, her fingertips on his scalp, washed over him now.

She sucked in her breath and her eyes grew darker. He watched as her lips softened in an incredibly inviting way.

But Lucy wasn't his type. And what he was feeling confused him. It wasn't simple lust, which he understood. This was something else. Something warmer, kind of friendship with hotter undertones. He wanted to take that last step, to kiss her and see if she'd taste as good as he thought she would.

But instead he stepped back. Apart from the fact that she wasn't his type, Lucy was a woman with a clearly defined agenda. She was looking for love in a pretty serious way, and it wasn't fair to waste her time.

He grabbed her hand instead. "Let's go."

She shot him a look that suggested she was feeling some confusing things, too. But her hand felt good in his and he was a way better friend to women than he was a boyfriend.

"STRIKE!" LUCY SHOT HER FISTS into the air and jumped up and down. She didn't seem to mind that her shirt rose as she jumped, displaying a nice strip of her midriff. Her skin was winter-in-the-north pale, and he liked the delicate whiteness of her skin. Her belly was taut, not body-builder ripped, but tight like she kept herself in shape.

Probably by bowling. The woman could certainly knock the pins down. Each time she acted as if it was her first strike ever, jumping up and down and doing a little victory dance that seriously messed with his concentration. Especially as her already short skirt rose when she jumped, revealing a nice pair of legs. Slender but muscular.

Maybe he hadn't been on any high school championship bowling team, but he was a natural athlete. He'd always been good at sports. He was also competitive. Couldn't seem to help himself. If there was a board with numbers on it and his name appeared on this board, he naturally wanted his number to be higher than his opponent's.

Even if the name on the board was a seriously goofy name. Like Leonardo.

He hadn't paid too much attention when Lucy had typed their names into the computerized scoreboard until he'd glanced up to see them listed as Mona Lisa and Leonardo.

"Leonardo?"

She grinned at him. "Can't have you being stalked by fans. So I decided we should use aliases."

"Good plan. Everybody will think those are our real names, for sure."

She shrugged. "Less embarrassing for you than if I kick the butt of a famous race car driver."

And that's when it became the determined aim of Leonardo to outscore, outstrike and basically annihilate Mona Lisa.

Mona Lisa was no pushover, though. It turned out that Lucy had quite a competitive streak of her own. She had a way of standing there, with her purple ball in her hand—she always waited for the purple one—studying the pins with fierce concentration, her tongue tapping her upper lip reflectively.

She'd stand there for ages, as though the pins weren't lined up in exactly, precisely the same way every time. As though there weren't a mechanical contraption that had no other purpose in life than to realign the pins in the exact same spots.

Still, each time she went to roll her ball down a lane she studied the ten pins. Finally, he couldn't stand it anymore. It was the tongue tapping that got him. It was way too sexy.

"It's not a chessboard, Mona Lisa. Those ten pins are in the same spots they were last time you knocked them all down."

She turned to him in surprise, looking as though he'd woken her from a nap. The bracelets on her wrist caught the light and flashed. "I know that. I'm visualizing. It's the secret of my success." She paused. "Not that I should tell you that. You'll probably steal the idea."

He rolled his gaze. Couldn't help himself. He visualized success all the time. It was the most basic rule of sports psychology. And Lucy thought using the visualization technique was original?

But as he started to formulate a smart remark he realized that what he'd been doing over the last few days was imagine nothing but failure. Visions played out in his head over and over of him making a fool of himself and of everybody who'd believed in him.

He'd had a dream last night where he'd been driving around the track at thirty miles an hour. His mother had passed him on the inside, waving cheerily.

From a golf cart.

In that way of dreams, nothing he did made him go any faster. A kid on roller blades had whizzed past. Then he'd watched an old man in a walker overtake him.

He woke in a cold sweat.

This was so not good.

Lucy had reminded him of the most basic rule of sports psychology, all right. One he'd apparently forgotten.

He needed to turn those negative images into positive ones.

By the time she shared this information with him, she was ahead by ten points and he was starting to think he'd better pick up his game.

She went back to her prethrow Zenlike state, then

folded in half slowly, pulling her hand back and sending her ball flying down the lane. Her eyes narrowed until they almost looked closed. He watched the ball roll straight and true, heard the inevitable crash and watched every one of those ten pins go flying.

She danced around once more, throwing her hands in the air, pumping those cheerleader's legs and yelling "Strike!"

"Isn't Mona Lisa supposed to sit around looking pretty and smiling mysteriously?"

Lucy sent him a most unmysterious grin. "That was so sixteenth century."

He had to grin back at her. He couldn't help it. Her simple enthusiasm was infectious.

Didn't mean he was going to let her win, though.

Getting into the condo, pulling her hand free and making the chilly air even worse for him. He knew not to wait until she walked to her own door, he watched her unlock her condo and go inside, and that killed me. When she gave one of those a little grin. I could.

She grinned to herself that she'd been throwing horns in the air as she headed for a table at NASCAR.

CHAPTER SIX

"OH, THAT WAS FUN," Lucy said, wondering when she'd enjoyed a day more. "My day started out crummy and ended up fantastic." They were parked outside her rental condo, where he'd insisted on driving her home.

"Even though I beat you at bowling?" He looked a little sheepish, as though he'd meant to let her win and hadn't been able to control his competitive drive.

She laughed. "I hardly ever get to play against anybody who's as good as me. And besides, I was winning until you stole my visualization idea."

Sawyer looked a lot more relaxed than he had at the track, she was happy to notice. "I had a lot of fun today too."

"Good." She reached for the door handle. This was it. She'd had a wonderful, magical day, even had got Sam to snap a photo of her with Sawyer at the track so she could show them all at NASCARfan.com and especially Dan Krankill that she'd had a great time in Daytona. Now she was going to have to go back to being one of the anonymous fans.

She'd had her moment as an insider. It had been fantastic.

She turned back. "Thanks for everything. And good luck tomorrow."

His relaxed expression disappeared as a crease formed between his brows. "You're going to be there, right? At the qualifying?"

"Sure. I'll be in the stands, but—"

"No. I want you in the pit box. Please, Lucy. I'll get you set up with a headset and everything so you can listen to what's going on."

He was so sweet. "You don't have to do this, Sawyer. I had a wonderful time today, but you don't have to look after me anymore. I'll be fine."

"But I won't."

"What are you talking about?"

"I don't know." He fiddled with the steering wheel. "Can't explain it, but I can relax around you. I start thinking I'm going to choke and you do something goofy that makes me laugh, or you remind me to visualize." He glanced up, looking serious. "I'm here right now because I take advantage of everything that helps me drive better. Even strategies that don't make sense. And I think I'll do better knowing you're in the pit box, so I'm asking you please to come be part of my team tomorrow."

"You're superstitious?"

"Heck, yeah. Other people have four-leaf clovers

or special medallions or some kind of trinket they believe in. Me, I've got the Mona Lisa."

Her spirits lifted like a helium balloon escaped from a tiny fist. "I would love to watch you from the pits. Yes."

Immediately, his expression relaxed again. "Okay. I'll see you tomorrow."

He leaned across and she figured he was going to kiss her cheek, but at the last minute he seemed to change his mind and, gripping her chin in his hand, pressed his lips briefly to hers.

He pulled away and she caught the silver gray blur of his eyes.

"'Night, Lucy."

"Good night."

She got out of the truck and pretty much floated into the condo building. All she could think was *Wow.* It was only a little dry-mouthed peck on the lips but she felt as if rockets had burst inside her head.

She couldn't even imagine what kissing Sawyer could be like if he actually put some effort into it.

Even as she tried to convince herself that he'd kissed her as he would a sister, she felt that there was something special between them.

Oh, as if.

He was a hot, young NASCAR driver and even though he enjoyed her company enough that he wanted her back with him tomorrow, he'd all but told her it was because of her skills in helping him fight his performance anxiety. It wasn't because he had romantic inclinations. She didn't have an outside chance with a man like Sawyer.

Except there was that kiss. As though his body was telling him something his brain didn't want to hear. She touched her fingertips to her lips. Since she'd first been kissed when she was fourteen years old—let's see, thirty-two years minus fourteen—she stood there for a moment doing the math in her head—eighteen years ago, she'd never experienced a kiss that left her quite so breathless.

But maybe Sawyer was an exceptional kisser and all women felt this effervescent after he kissed them.

Even though he'd said he didn't have a current girlfriend, she wondered what kind of women he usually dated. Fortunately, he was a public figure, so that kind of information was readily available.

Instead of heading up to her suite, she detoured to an alcove, where several computers were set up.

The condo building wasn't busy this time of night, so she had no trouble getting a computer and logging onto the Internet.

After ten minutes she pretty much wished she hadn't.

Not only had Sawyer been photographed with far too many women, they were all in a different league than Lucy. These were the goddesses she worked with. The ones who wore the designer gowns that flowed over their perfect bodies. They were six feet tall with huge eyes and dramatic cheekbones. Each of them had been blessed with glorious combinations of genes. Lucy was five foot five, with nothing particularly remarkable about her. She was the one on her knees before the goddesses, pinning up their gowns and fastening the straps of their designer shoes.

She'd never for one moment felt jealous of the supermodels she dressed. Not until now, when she realized that was the kind of woman Sawyer belonged with, not quirky, not-nearly-perfect Lucy.

The worst blow of all came when she read the caption beneath a photograph of him and an L.A. starlet at some fund-raiser. Sawyer was in a tuxedo, looking as at home in the formal wear as he did in his uniform. He was grinning at the camera, his arm around the gorgeous blond actress. The photo was part of a magazine feature called *Hot Guys Under Thirty*.

The photo cutline read: At twenty-seven, NASCAR hottie Sawyer Patton is on the fast track with his female fan base, including soap opera star, Laci Ridge, who, when asked for one word to describe Sawyer, smiled saucily and said, "sensational."

Lucy shut off the computer with a jab of her finger. Sensational hottie Sawyer Patton was not only out of her league in the dating department, but he was five years younger.

She felt like an ancient old crone as she took the

elevator up to her floor and entered her condo. Her very lonely condo.

For some reason, she'd brought the book her Auntie Grace had given her to Florida with her, and it sat on the coffee table mocking her.

Last Chance for Love.

Had she ever really had a first or second or third chance? When she reviewed her record, Lucy realized she'd never been with anyone who came closer than warm liking.

She was thirty-two years old and she'd never been in love.

Now she wondered how any man would be able to compete with a guy she'd only met this morning, but who seemed to combine all those qualities she'd secretly always wanted.

He was kind, funny, talented and down-to-earth. She loved the ambition and hard work that had brought him success in a tough sport, and she loved the way he could relax and goof around with her. Even though she wasn't the hottest woman on the block, Sawyer hadn't once checked out other women when he'd been with her. Apart from all that, he was gorgeous and had a great physique.

Oh, Lord. It was as though she'd fallen in love with a movie star she'd seen on the big screen. For a sensible woman of thirty-two years, she'd just gone and developed the hugest crush of her life.

She threw open the sliding doors to the patio to

let in the sound of the waves down below, then plopped down on the couch and grabbed the book.

Okay, so even though the Dan Krankill thing had been a disaster, the book had given her a nudge in the right direction.

What was the next bit of advice?

Chapter Two: What is Your Mirror Telling You?

Lucy's bad mood deepened. She knew perfectly well what her mirror would tell her. The same story it had been telling her for months. She was ordinary. And she was aging. A few tiny lines had started to form around her eyes and she was almost positive she'd seen a gray hair a couple of weeks ago.

She skimmed through the chapter. Yeah, yeah. She knew all this stuff. Dress in styles that flattered her, make sure her makeup and hair were up-to-date. She was in the fashion business. She knew all about style. But a sense of style wasn't going to add six inches to her height or blade her cheekbones or take the craziness out of her hair.

Lucy had always enjoyed physical exercise and she ate sensibly so she figured her body was as good as it was ever going to be without surgery. She liked her body. It wasn't a ten on anyone's scale, but she felt at home with it. She only wished some of the gorgeous creatures she dressed felt as at home in theirs.

And wasn't that the irony of feminine beauty?

Having speed read her way through chapter two, she flipped to chapter three.

Chapter Three: Be Mysterious.

Mysterious? Men, the book explained, don't want to know all about you on a first date. Drop hints about your exotic travels or your fascinating job. Don't give him your résumé and memoirs the first day. And never, ever, the book warned her, tell him you are reading a book called *Last Chance for Love.* "Remember, you want to appear mysterious, not desperate."

She slammed the book shut.

That was it.

She'd pretty much broken every rule of chapter three within the first hour of knowing Sawyer. She put her hands over her face, squeezing her palms against her cheeks as she recalled how she'd told him all about her job, Dan Krankill and the Book That Had Ruined Her Life.

And that was within the first thirty minutes of their relationship.

She might as well give up now and put away her foolish dreams. She was as likely to end up with Sawyer Patton as she'd have been to end up with Randy Galliano, the guy she'd adored through most of high school. Even though she'd written Lucy Galliano and Mrs. Randy Galliano about a thousand times in various school binders, nothing but teasing from her girlfriends had ever come of it.

She should scrawl Lucy Patton on her binder and get it over with.

Never able to stay down for long, her mood lightened as she prepared to get into the huge king-size bed all by herself.

Naturally, she was grown up now and a feminist who planned to keep her own name after marriage, but she had to admit, Lucy Patton was a pretty cute name.

CHAPTER SEVEN

SAWYER COULDN'T BELIEVE he was finally here. Qualifying for his first NASCAR Sprint Cup Series race. He felt pumped, a little nervous but mostly excited.

There were two race-off duels, twenty-nine cars in each. Only forty-three spots on race day, so his performance today was critical.

He'd slept better than he could have imagined after the crazy night of bowling. Lucy's reminder to visualize a great ride had helped him a lot but even more, the quick kiss they'd shared had steadied him.

And how weird was that?

He had no idea why something so insignificant should have such an impact on him, but every time he thought of that quick brush of his lips against hers, he felt calm. Centered. Grounded. All those words that added up to feeling as relaxed as a guy in his position could be.

A few of the senior drivers made sure to pat him on the back, share a joke or a lighthearted insult. He felt part of something he'd dreamed of since he had watched his first race on TV back when he was a kid.

There wasn't a full crowd in the stands like there would be on race day, but there were plenty of spectators, and when his name was announced, he even got a nice cheer.

Now all he had to do was drive well.

He glanced over at Lucy, and that wonderful sense of calm came over him once more. She looked as bright as the poppies his mom grew in the backyard, with a short-sleeved red shirt and a pair of jeans that fit her snug little body perfectly. He gave her a thumbs-up. She blew him a kiss and even though he couldn't hear the tinkle of her bangle bracelets, he saw them moving like a silver waterfall and imagined their sound.

It was time.

The next hour was pretty much a blur. He started out cautious, determined not to act like a hothead and do something stupid. But as the laps peeled away, he felt his adrenaline even out and all the reasons he loved this sport roared in to kick his performance up a notch.

He loved driving, loved the mechanical skills involved and the almost spooky mental part of guessing what another driver would do before he made a move, and when to pass, when to hold, when to tuck behind a car and ride its draft, when to pull out and take his chance.

His mom didn't pass him in her golf cart, no kids on skateboards made him eat their dust, no old guys in walkers; he was neither the fastest driver nor the slowest, finishing nicely in the middle, exactly as he'd hoped. He had his spot lined up for the big race. He couldn't believe the rush of relief that washed over him.

Since he was a rookie, there was naturally quite a bit of media interest in him.

He pulled himself out of the car hot and sweaty and desperate for a long, cool shower. Instead, he hauled off his helmet, did his best to look like what he'd done was no big deal. But all his excitement had to go somewhere.

He saw Lucy. She was standing behind the reporters who were waiting for him and her face was shining with excitement and pride. He didn't even think. He acted on the same instincts he'd been relying on since his first go-kart race in his teens.

He walked right up to her, hauled her up off her toes and kissed her long and hard.

He was sweaty, probably smelly and wearing a uniform, but she didn't seem to mind. She fit right into him, and her mouth connected with his like it had last night. Only better.

Little sparks exploded in his blood. He tightened his arms around her, deepened the kiss. She made a tiny sound of satisfaction, low in her throat. He was so stoked right now he could hardly stand it. When he set her back down on the ground, she looked both flustered and happy.

"Thanks for the great advice," he said, then turned to face the reporters.

And became aware that his spontaneous kiss had been recorded for posterity. A network crew were filming, a still photographer was clicking away and a digital recorder had the material to stream his impulsive kiss on line in seconds.

Oh, well. He couldn't worry about that.

He tried to focus on what he'd say to the media, but the first question shot at him had nothing to do with the race.

"Who's the pretty lady?" asked the network reporter, standing with a cameraman who was still filming. Sawyer drew her forward. "This is Lucy." And please don't let them ask him for her last name because he'd forgotten it.

But nobody asked for her last name. "Is she your girlfriend?" the gal from the online news feed asked him. Sawyer wasn't yet fast on his feet when it came to interviews and all the media training he'd taken hadn't prepared him for a situation like this.

"My girlfriend? Lucy?" He'd just laid a good one on a woman and all the world and his sisters would be able to view it within the hour. What was he supposed to say that wouldn't reflect badly on Lucy? She was a nice woman who'd helped him a lot. He didn't want anybody thinking she was a quick hookup. That she wasn't important to him.

So he did the only thing he could think of. He said, "Yes, yes, she is."

If the news had surprised him, it had pretty

much stunned Lucy, who had clearly never had any media training, since she allowed the shock to show on her face.

Fortunately, the reporters were more interested in his driving than his love life and the next question was one he was well prepared to answer. "How did it feel coming 12th in your qualifying race?"

"We were hoping to end up in the middle and we did. Everybody pulled together, the car was running great, the spotter did a fantastic job and I had a little beginner's luck." He grinned at the camera, trying to look easy and relaxed. "I'm really happy with the result."

"How do you feel going into the race?"

He caught Lucy's eye. "I feel sensational."

But Lucy had gone suddenly pale and was making jerky movements with her head, as if she had a tic. Had he shocked her so much with his blurted comment that she was his girlfriend?

Finally, he figured that she was trying to draw his attention to something behind him. A horrible premonition came over him.

Please, let it not be…

"Great job, son."

"I am so proud of you, baby!"

"Good going, bro."

"Not too shabby, Patty Cake Man."

…his family.

CHAPTER EIGHT

LUCY THOUGHT SHE'D hit her embarrassment peak when Sawyer had lied to the world and network television and said she was his girlfriend. It was the panicked expression on his face that had done her in. He wanted her to be his girlfriend like he wanted to forget how to drive.

That should have been the worst moment, but then she'd glanced behind Sawyer and seen a group of people she recognized from her Internet research of the previous night. He'd now claimed she was his girlfriend in front of his family, who were all looking at her with interest and, from the younger Pattons, a big dose of skepticism. They knew their brother was a babe magnet. They must be wondering what he was doing with her.

His face was a comical blend of horror and bravado, and if she were watching other people play out this farce, she'd have been pretty amused. As it was, all she felt was an urge to flee, far and fast.

But Sawyer had other ideas. He took her arm and

pulled her forward. "Lucy," he said with fake heartiness, "I want you to meet my family."

"Hi, I'm Lucy Vanderwal," she said, as she stuck her hand out at random, wanting only to cover the fact that she was pretty sure that once again, Sawyer didn't remember his girlfriend's last name.

Sawyer's father took pity on her waving hand and shook it in his meaty paw. He looked as though he'd once played football. He was a big, muscular man, and a good-looking one, too. "Vanderwal," he said. "Is that Dutch?"

"Sure is, like the tulip." Oh, God, could she sound any more inane?

"I love tulips. I'm the gardener in the family," said Sawyer's mother, whose tall body and arresting features suggested she might once have modeled. Or been a beauty queen. She was also kind enough to try and put Lucy at ease. Sawyer must have inherited his good nature from her. "I'm Cheryl, and my husband is Bill." She gestured to the two women standing beside Bill. "And these are Sawyer's sisters, Roberta and Emily."

"Hi." She shook their hands, as well. Roberta was gorgeous and willowy like their mother, but Emily was only about her own height, and she had freckles. She was cute, but no knock-out. Lucy felt pathetically grateful that there was one mere mortal in the family.

Sisters were pretty much the same everywhere in Lucy's experience and these two were no exception. "You didn't tell us you had a girlfriend," Roberta said.

"How did you two meet? And when?" demanded Emily.

But Sawyer had had a few minutes to prepare for the expected onslaught and he said, "Hey, forget my love life for a second. What did you think of the qualifying?"

"Oh, honey, we missed the beginning. We're so sorry. I told your father we needed to get an earlier start this morning, but you know how he is." She turned to Lucy and mouthed, "Always thinks he knows everything."

"You read the map wrong or we would have had plenty of time."

"Look," Sawyer said, "I've got to shower and have a meeting with the team. How about we all have dinner together? We can barbecue at my motor home."

"I'll bring all the fixings," his mother replied. "What time do you want us?"

"How about six o'clock?"

"All right. I guess we can live without you for a couple of hours. But poor Lucy. You'll be so bored. Why don't you come with us, honey? And we can get to know you better."

She had no idea what to say. "Oh, well..." she managed before Sawyer interrupted. "I need Lucy to stay with me." When his whole family looked at him strangely, he added, "you know, young love."

"Right," said Roberta.

"Well, all right then," said his mother. "See you at six. Oh, and thank your lovely assistant for arranging passes for us. This is so exciting!"

Having been given directions to Sawyer's trailer, the Patton family headed off and Sawyer let out a breath. "I am so sorry about that. I got caught off guard, didn't know what to say. I mean, I didn't want anybody thinking we'd just hooked up or something. I guess I could have said you were a friend, but they all saw me kissing you and—" He ran his hand through his already disheveled hair. "I wasn't thinking, I guess."

She tried not to wish that he wasn't quite so freaked out by his accidental announcement. Maybe she was half a decade older than him and not some six-foot bombshell, but still, he might have pretended to like the idea simply to make her feel better.

"That's okay. We'll tell your family the truth tonight. I'm sure they'll understand. You were under a lot of pressure and you blurted out the first thing you could think of. Anyone could do that." Though not often on TV.

"You're right. I feel bad, though. I screwed up. Here you are looking for a nice guy to settle down with and I'm acting like you're with me. Some friend."

You're a nice guy is what she wanted to say, but instead she gave him her best smile. "I think it might be a good thing. If people think I was your girlfriend, it will give them a reason to take a second look at me." And, she reminded herself, she'd be mysterious while she was at it, and not go telling all the details of her life the first hour she met someone.

"Speaking of which, I should go find a sports bar and hang out for a while. When that clip gets played, I'll be a minor celebrity."

He frowned suddenly. "You're not going trolling to any sports bar. Not when you're supposed to be my girlfriend. Think of my reputation."

"Well then, what do you suggest I do?"

"Stay with me. I know lots of nice guys. I'll introduce you around."

"As what?" She smiled at him sweetly.

"Oh, right." He squinted against the sun. "I really did goof up, didn't I?"

"Yep. You did."

"I'll make it up to you, Lucy. I promise. But can it wait until tomorrow?"

"Sure. I think I'd better go find something to do for a bit, though. I'll see you later."

"Hey, I know I screwed up and everything, but do you mind hanging around?" She glanced at him in surprise. "I know it sounds weird, but I just feel better when you're around."

"Okay. But don't get used to it. I'm only here until Monday, you know."

"I don't know what magic you have. You're like the NASCAR whisperer or something. You can relax me when I'm tense. I have a feeling I'll do a lot better on Sunday if you're around."

What could she do? So she wasn't the love of his life, she was the NASCAR whisperer. Still, hanging around the track with Sawyer was better than sitting around in her condo reading more of that stupid book. "Okay."

"I BOUGHT STEAK AND potatoes and all the fixings, and some mushroom burgers in case Lucy is a vegetarian," Cheryl said as Sawyer's family arrived for the impromptu barbecue.

"That was nice of you," said Lucy.

Sawyer bristled. "What do you mean? Does she look like a vegetarian?"

"What's wrong with being a vegetarian?" Lucy asked.

"You can never tell," Cheryl said at the same time.

"Son, with your track record, we never know what we're getting into."

His mother nodded and leaned closer to Lucy. "I don't want to pry, but is there any twelve-step program you're in that we should be aware of? Bill bought some beer, but if that's a problem for you—"

"No! No. It's fine. I don't have any addictions. I eat meat. I'm a pretty regular person."

His mother's face relaxed into a big smile.

"Bonanza!" Sawyer yelled, and she watched as a black bullet with floppy ears launched himself at the driver. He jumped around, barking excitedly, knocking over a folding chair and licking every bit of Sawyer he could reach with his big tongue.

Then she was introduced to the dog, who they claimed could shake a paw, but he was so excited he jumped up and put his black paws on her thighs instead. Then he raced back to Sawyer.

Cheryl sat down beside Lucy in one of the folding chairs she and Sawyer had set up in front of his fancy trailer. "I can't tell you what a relief that is. You know I love Sawyer, but that boy has the most awful taste in women. They're all crazy or addicted or have an eating disorder or something. The only thing they have in common is they're all beautiful. That's why I had a feeling you'd be different."

Lucy tried to hide her smile as Cheryl realized what she'd said and slapped a well-manicured hand over her mouth. "That did not come out at all the way I meant it to. You're lovely and have such a vivacious face and friendly personality. I only meant—"

"It's okay. I know exactly what you meant. I work with fashion models and believe me, I know I'm not in their league."

His mother leaned closer. "Are they all as crazy as the ones Sawyer's brought home?"

"No. Of course not. There are a lot of really wonderful women in the fashion world. But it's an incredibly stressful job and it's way too easy to get caught up in a lifestyle that's not exactly healthy."

"I'm so glad you understand. So, tell me, what do you do in fashion?"

Lucy found herself telling Cheryl Patton about her job and hearing all about Cheryl's work as a speech therapist in return. She also heard more than she wanted to about what a good son Sawyer was and all the sweet things he'd ever done.

Within ten minutes Lucy knew that Sawyer might not think she was good enough to be his girlfriend, but his mother had other ideas.

The men cooked the steaks and potatoes while the women prepared salads and chatted. Lucy found herself warming to all of his family even as she felt they were sizing her up.

She kept waiting for Sawyer to mention his blunder on television and tell them all that she wasn't his girlfriend, but every time there was a logical opportunity he didn't take it.

After dinner was over and they were drinking coffee, Cheryl sat beside her again. When Sawyer's mom started asking if she planned to have children in the future, Lucy knew his former girlfriends must have been really bad. The poor woman was latching on to her like a daughter-in-law life raft.

"I love kids," she said. Sawyer must have overheard their conversation, for he was sitting on her other side, rubbing Bonanza's head, not currently talking to anyone. "But I think Sawyer has something he needs to tell you."

"What is it?" Cheryl asked, leaning across Lucy to address her son. Her eyes widened as she looked from one to the other, "You're not—"

Sawyer looked exasperated. "No. Of course not. Lucy only meant that I love kids too, but then you already know that."

What was he doing? She nudged his knee.

He ignored her.

She stepped on his toe. He winced but ignored that, too.

Finally, she said, "Sawyer, can you help me with something in the kitchen?"

"I'll help," said Emily.

"I think she wants to talk to him alone," Roberta explained.

"Oh, right. Sorry."

Now they'd made a big deal of it, she felt her cheeks heating. "It'll just take a sec," she mumbled.

Sawyer followed her into the motor home and shut the door, but that didn't work because the dog started to howl piteously, so they had to open the door again and let him in, too. As they hit the small living area, she could feel the eyes of all his family burning holes through the metal walls.

"What are you doing?" she asked Sawyer.

"Nothing."

"I know. You're doing nothing to disabuse your family of the idea that I am your…" she couldn't even say the word. She suddenly felt peculiar. "You know."

"Would it be so bad?"

"Would what be so bad?"

Bonanza stood between them, his head turning from side to side as they spoke, as though following the conversation.

"You being my girlfriend?"

Those were words she would love to hear, but she felt as if there should be a little more romance be-hind them and a little less calculation. "You don't see me that way," she reminded him.

"You don't know that. Anyhow, they all like you so much and nobody's trying to set me up with some nice friend of theirs or giving me a hard time because my girlfriend's a fruitcake. Makes a nice change from most family barbecues. It's very relaxing."

"You know, I realize that when we met I may have given you the impression that I am pathetic, but I'm really not that pathetic." She felt angry and hurt and stupid all at the same time. What had she expected? He kept her around because she helped him with his stress. That she could take, but to keep her as a fake girlfriend to shield him from his interfering family? Oh, no.

She turned to the door. She really had to get out of here.

The dog whined and bumped against her side. She thought maybe he'd picked up on her distress.

"Good dog," she said, patting his head.

Sawyer caught her arm. "Hey, I don't think you're

pathetic. I think you're great. Why don't we give this thing a try?"

She crossed her arms over her chest. "Sawyer, I am thirty-two years old. Five years older than you."

"You're four years older than me."

Fury erupted that he would lie to her about his age. "You're twenty-seven. I read it on the Internet!"

A slight grin lightened his expression. "Checking up on me, eh? Well, you must have read an old article. I've had a birthday since then."

"Happy birthday. So I'm four years older than you."

"I don't care about that, Lucy. You told me you were over thirty in the diner, remember?"

"You forgot to mention that you were only twenty-seven."

"Twenty-eight, and what does age matter? My mom's right. You're the nicest girl I've dated since…" He seemed to do a quick review of his whole romantic life. "Since ever."

"We aren't dating," she reminded him. "And I can't play games, Sawyer. I'm not made that way. Let's be honest. I'm not hot enough for you."

"Why don't you let me decide if you're hot enough for me, huh?"

He closed in before she could get the door open and ran his hands up her arms to her shoulders. "I don't know about you, but when I touch you I feel nothing but heat." His voice had a lazy quality, like he had all day to do nothing but think about kissing her, maybe one day get around to actually doing it. "The kissing thing has me thinking."

She watched his mouth moving, coming closer to hers, fascinated by the way his strong arms felt on her shoulders, by the way he smelled, of his shower gel and shampoo and fast-driving man. "Thinking what?" Was that her voice? That soft, sexy purr.

"Thinking that the first time was a quick goodnight kiss that left me feeling as if we'd exchanged a deep soul kiss, and the second time was on TV in front of a bunch of people and it rocked my world. I'm wondering how we'd be in private without an audience."

"You're forgetting your family. I believe they are all trying to peek in the windows."

"Forget my family," he said, and then claimed her mouth with his.

As he tasted her, toyed with her mouth, brought her closer until she was pressed against him, her arms wrapping around his neck of their own accord, she completely forgot about his family.

Which wasn't easy, since they were cheering.

CHAPTER NINE

WHAT WAS SHE SUPPOSED to do? Sawyer was looking at her as though he truly wanted her in his romantic life, his entire family was cheering them on—in the literal, noisy, Go Team, Go! sense. Of course she agreed to stay around. But deep inside, she felt nervous.

Lucy knew herself. She could far too easily fall for this guy. What if she helped him build up his confidence, which she could see wouldn't take long, and then he dumped her?

Still, she wasn't going to ruin this great day for him, or his family. So she'd let herself believe, at least for this magical week, and when Daytona was over, she suspected her stint as his girlfriend would be, too, and she'd have to be okay with that.

In the meantime, she'd study that silly book. She had to admit, chapter one had worked out pretty well. She'd gone where the men were and found herself a fine one. If only she'd read chapter three before blabbing all her personal stuff, maybe Sawyer would have seen her as more than a pity project.

Next time she was keeping her mystery. And when she thought about it, maybe her style, while very much her own, wasn't exactly alluring to men.

But the idea of changing so much of herself to please a man was so depressing, she couldn't even think about it right now.

As they walked back out to where his family was waiting, she tried to act cool. But of course that wasn't going to happen. His family wouldn't let her.

Cheryl came forward and touched Lucy on the shoulder. "There's nothing like kissing to solve an argument, is there? Bill and I still do it. And one thing I'm sure I don't have to tell you two, never go to bed angry."

Lucy was startled. "Oh, we haven't—"

Sawyer interrupted her. "You're so right, Mom. Lucy and I absolutely believe that, don't we, honey?"

"Well, yes, theoretically."

"Come on," he said, dragging her to the table, where his mom had set up a plate of cupcakes. "Let's get some dessert. You know how I love cupcakes."

"Why are you doing this?" she asked him in a furious undertone while she pretended to choose between chocolate with pink frosting and a lemon cupcake. "You let your parents think we're sleeping together. The way you talk, we're practically married."

"Are you kidding me? Have you seen my family?

They are the nosiest, most interfering people on the planet. I'm buying us a little space is all."

"I like them," she said. In fact, it wasn't until later that she realized the reason she enjoyed them so much was that they reminded her of her own family. Drive-you-crazy interfering but also the kind of loving, caring people you couldn't stay mad at, even if they kept butting into your business.

"I like them, too, but I'm under enough pressure right now without them getting involved in my love life."

"So, I'm your smoke screen?"

He let out an irritated breath. Ignoring the cupcakes, he announced, "Bonanza needs a run. We're going to take him for a walk." He grabbed the wet tennis ball the dog had arrived with and the three of them took off.

The drivers and their families were all staying in the inner track area set aside for them, and as they wandered around, he waved and said hi to a few of the families. Bonanza had to be called back to heel every time he smelled food in somebody else's place.

"I swear, Lucy, you're going to drive me crazy. Why are you so determined that nothing could work between us?"

"I'm not your usual type."

"Can a man not have more than one type?"

"I suppose. But our relationship only started because you took pity on me."

"Excuse me. As I recall, you beat me up and bought me a milkshake to apologize."

She appreciated him putting it that way. It made her sound a lot more powerful than she really was, but they both knew the truth.

"And, I'm not mysterious."

He threw back his head and laughed. "I will give you that, Lucy. You are definitely not mysterious. But you know, I like that about you. I can't stand being with women where you never know where you stand, who say things they don't mean, or don't say anything at all and you're supposed to figure out what you did that made them mad." He shook his head. "Human beings are complicated enough. I don't see why people have to make it even harder."

She sighed. "I know. But being straightforward and uncomplicated hasn't done me much good."

"Come on. You can be as mysterious and complicated as you like around my parents. By which I mean, let's not tell them we only met yesterday, okay?"

Had they only known each other a day? She knew it was true, but it felt as though Sawyer had been part of her life for ages. He'd come into her life so easily, she had a feeling it was going to be a lot harder for her to let him go.

"All right. I think you're a terrible person to lie to your family, but all right."

He hugged her, then took her hand. As the dog

bounded ahead, chasing scents and galloping after his ball every time Sawyer threw it, they strolled around the motor homes and made their slow way back. His hand felt nice linked with hers, their palms warm against each other, fingers interlocked. This was what she wanted, this connection. Maybe one of these days she'd find it with one of her own kind. A mere mortal.

WHEN HER DOOR BUZZER sounded late the next morning, Lucy had to wonder what she'd thrown herself into. Sawyer's younger sister had suggested they have lunch together while her brother was in sponsorship meetings and, unable to think of an excuse, she'd said yes.

Afterward, she thought of ten things she could have said. A previously booked mani and pedi, a massage, a hair appointment…there were so many possibilities, but of course her mind had been blank. The sad thing was that she'd liked Emily immediately and under normal circumstances would have been happy to get to know her better, but with her extremely strange girlfriend/no-girlfriend status in Sawyer's life she'd just as soon avoid any intimate tête-à-têtes with his family.

A significant glance from him as they'd made their plans had reminded her in no uncertain terms that she was to stick to the script. Even though the script hadn't even been written yet. She supposed she'd improvise and then let Sawyer in on whatever she'd come up with so their lies matched.

It was exhausting.

She wore a summer dress from a designer line that was two years old. The dress was floral and funky and with some chunky sandals and a dozen of her favorite bangles gave her confidence.

Sawyer's sister wanted to come up and check out the condo. "Oh, wow. Look at the view. And you've got so much room. No wonder you wanted to stay here instead of in Sawyer's motor home."

"I like my own space." Plus, there was the tiny detail that she hadn't even known Sawyer when she booked the place. She'd been planning on a romance with a different guy.

She was so certain she was going to have a pounding headache by the time lunch was over that she'd slipped a couple of painkillers into her bag.

"I Googled restaurants and found a really cute-sounding place near here with seafood and salads and stuff. Does that sound okay?"

"Yes. Of course. How efficient of you."

Emily grinned, and in that moment looked very much like her brother. "I know. I'm a foodie, so I always pick the restaurants in our family. I wanted to be a chef but it seemed like I'd spend way too much time doing boring stuff."

"What did you end up doing?"

"I'm in PR. I'm with a big agency and they let me

work on some of our food and beverage accounts. I'm hoping to make F and B my specialty. In the meantime, I cook for family and friends."

They left the condo and took the elevator down to the main level.

"Next time you're in California you'll have to come to my place and I'll cook for you."

"I'd like that." Not that it was likely to happen, but she'd love to get to know this fun woman better.

The restaurant Emily had chosen was wonderful, with a bright pastel décor and food that was fresh and simply prepared. Lucy only wished she could settle down enough to enjoy her meal.

Instead, as they faced each other over a small table near open windows that looked out to the beach, Sawyer's sister launched right into the interrogation she'd dreaded, "So, how did you two meet?"

"What did Sawyer tell you?"

"Nothing! He drives me crazy most of the time. He said you'd tell us everything."

And thank you, Sawyer. "Well, there's not much to tell." She'd had all night to come up with a plausible story that wasn't too far from the truth, knowing she couldn't out and out lie to Sawyer's family. "I'm a racing fan and I got to know Sawyer through a fan site. NASCARfan.com." Which was the truth.

"Oh, that's so cool. Like *You've Got Mail.*"

She thought of the Dan Krankill fiasco. "Yes, sort of like that."

"Anyhow, we met in person and I liked him right away." She grinned at the avid face across from her. "You know what one of the first things he said to me was?"

"What?"

"That I reminded him of you."

His sister tilted her head to one side. "I can sort of see that. Not that we look alike or anything, but you seem like you give as good as you get. Sawyer really needs that in his life."

"Really? I feel like sometimes I'm too ordinary. I'm not a leggy supermodel type or specially smart or rich or anything. I'm so…" she shrugged "…plain."

"Are you kidding me? I thought Mom was going to break down and weep with joy when she got to know you last night. I'm serious."

Lucy had to smile. "I liked your mom."

"You have no idea. Okay, I'm going to tell you the truth about Sawyer, and you know I'm only doing this because I love him and I think you're good for him, so listen up."

She leaned forward. "Okay. I'm listening."

Their food came and for a few minutes they busied themselves with tasting the seafood salads they'd both ordered.

"You may have noticed that Sawyer is kind of competitive. And I don't just mean on the race track."

"Oh, I know. We went bowling one time and for most of the game I was in the lead. It was killing him."

"Wow. You must be a good bowler. Sawyer's killer at everything."

"I was on a championship team in school, but you're right. He still beat me. So, yes, I've seen first-hand how competitive he can be."

"When we were growing up, Sawyer was maybe not the absolute best-looking guy in his grade, but he was up there. Girls always liked him. But, you know how guys are. They not only want the hottest girls, they want the girls the other guys all want. To Sawyer it became another competition. A game."

"He thinks of women as a game?" It was worse than she'd imagined.

"I'm getting to that. He used to. See, he never looked for women who genuinely interested him. He went for the hard-to-get girls, mostly for the excitement of the chase, if you want my opinion."

She munched thoughtfully for a minute on her organic greens. "Then, once he'd got these girls to go out with him, he'd usually lose interest. And frankly, most of the women he's dated didn't have much going for them but their looks. Not that I mean to be dissing other women. It's more like he didn't bother to look any closer than their faces and bodies. Like to whether they were maybe crazy or had some kind of other problem."

"He seems too smart to fall for a pretty face."

"Smart when he wants to be. But in some ways he never grew up. I mean, he started playing with cars and trucks when he was three and he's still doing it."

Lucy had to laugh.

"It's the same with women. He never graduated from his selection process in junior high." She grinned. "Until now."

"You mean, me?"

"You, Lucy Vanderwal, are the proof that my big brother Sawyer has finally grown up. It's like a boy chose those other women. And a man chose you."

Lucy would have felt thrilled, lighthearted and over the moon if it were true and Sawyer really had chosen her. And based on what Emily was saying, she'd be a fantastic choice for him. She challenged him and supported him and, apart from that horrible Dan Krankill episode, she wasn't crazy. But the truth was he hadn't chosen her. Her four-years-younger guy really was still a boy.

"Anyhow, I guess we're all hoping you'll stick around."

"Thanks." Now if she could only convince Sawyer of that idea.

CHAPTER TEN

"OH, SAWYER, SHE'S LOVELY," his mom gushed as they caught up in a brief phone call between sponsorship meetings. His car wasn't plastered with decals yet, but the sponsorships were coming in. If he made a good showing Sunday, he suspected he'd have even more.

"You really liked Lucy?" It was a strange and novel experience to have his family actually approve of one of his girlfriends. He'd always figured he didn't care one way or the other what they thought, but he had to admit it was nice to have the support. But then, who could help liking Lucy? She was fun and surprising.

Especially when it came to kissing. He couldn't believe the heat the two of them generated when they got started. Seemed like every time they did, they had to stop, which had only left him craving more.

She felt right in his arms, not being too tall, and when he wrapped his arms around her he didn't feel as if he was going to crush her bones. She had enough padding that he could enjoy the feel of her without worrying about breakage.

Sure, she'd never grace the cover of a fashion mag, or have her own TV show, but he didn't really care about that stuff anyway.

The only thing that was starting to get on his nerves was this weird obsession she had with age.

No, that wasn't the thing that was bothering him the most. That would be that she didn't seem to believe he could be serious about her.

Maybe because he hadn't been at first, but the minute the shock wore off after he'd blabbed to the world that she was his girlfriend, he realized he was speaking from the smart part of his brain, the one he didn't access very often where women were concerned.

Maybe they wouldn't end up together forever. Who knew, when they'd only met a few days ago, but he was positive she'd be a lot more fun to hang around with than most of his former girlfriends.

"The only thing is, Mom, that Lucy's a couple of years older than I am and I think she's looking to get married pretty soon. She's a forever kind of girl. You know?"

"Of course she is. I'll tell you a secret. I was that kind of girl, too. And your father, well, let's just say you take after him in a lot of ways. I think I was the first girl he'd ever gone out with who got him to think about the future."

"I don't know. I don't want to give her false expectations."

"Honey, Lucy doesn't seem like a stupid woman. Why don't you let her decide if you're worth wasting her time on?"

"Are you calling your only son a waste of time?"

She laughed. "I think, for the first time in a long while, you aren't wasting your time with a woman."

It was something to think about.

He thought about Lucy and him when they played an impromptu game of hide and seek with Bonanza. Who had time to worry about Sunday when the world's craziest woman and the world's craziest dog were both keeping him running and his mind occupied?

He thought about Lucy when another driver and his family invited them over and he saw how good she was with people, especially the kids, who took to her immediately.

Saturday night he only wanted Lucy around. Everyone seemed to understand, including Lucy, who, for once, didn't argue. She showed up at his motor home, where they ate a simple dinner of salad, fish and rice, then walked Bonanza.

They were in the middle of a race track and it was never completely quiet. People were outside talking and laughing, and he imagined the numbers of fans stretched out from here to the farthest campgrounds and filling the motels and hotels of Daytona, doing pretty much the same as the drivers were doing. Relaxing and getting ready for the big day tomorrow.

The dog was happily chasing his ball, something he'd do twenty-four seven and never tire. After it got really slobbery, Lucy refused to throw it anymore. Even though Bonanza helpfully dropped it at her feet and looked at her with pleading in his liquid brown eyes.

"She throws like a girl, anyway," Sawyer reminded the dog, chucking the ball a lot farther than she could. Still, Bonanza wanted her to have her chance at the game and came right back and dropped the saliva-sodden tennis ball, now liberally coated with flecks of dirt and gravel, at her feet.

Even when he leaned down to retrieve and throw the ball, he never let go of Lucy's hand.

When they returned to his motor home, it was getting late. He knew she was going to make noises about leaving and knew he didn't want her to go.

Determined to stall her, he said, "So, do you have any more relaxation ideas for me? More visualizing or chanting mantras or something?"

The look she gave him was so open and sweet he wanted to pull her into his arms.

She said, "This is a very old technique. You know how in the Middle Ages, during jousting tournaments, a lady would give her knight a token so he knew she supported him?"

He nodded. If he hadn't read it in history books, he'd certainly seen the custom in movies.

She reached up and slipped the blue silk scarf

she'd worn with a V-necked T-shirt-type top and white jeans. Her bangles jingled as she slipped the silk from around her neck and presented it to him. It was still warm from her body and he knew that if he raised it to his nose it would hold her fragrance.

The movement hadn't been in any way provocative, and yet he thought watching her untie that silk from around her neck was the sexiest thing he'd ever seen.

"Thanks." He dug through a kitchen drawer until he found a permanent marker. "Would you sign it for me?"

She giggled. "Sure."

He watched her tongue tap her upper lip for a minute or two while she concentrated. Then she leaned over and carefully wrote on one end of the scarf.

I believe in you.

Love, Lucy

He read the words and felt something shift inside him and snap quietly into place.

He pulled her into his arms and kissed her, softly at first, then more deeply as he felt her respond. "Don't leave," he whispered. He didn't add, *I need you,* but he suspected she knew that already.

"No," she said softly. "I won't." And raised her lips to his.

CHAPTER ELEVEN

"COULDN'T ASK FOR A finer day for racing," the announcers were saying as Sunday dawned bright and clear. And it was true. Dry weather, sunny but not hot, no wind to speak of. It was a perfect Daytona day.

Sawyer had Lucy's scarf tucked beneath his uniform, and simply knowing it was there kept him centered.

He kept thinking about her during the race. Oh, not obsessively. He had a lot on his mind, listening to his spotter, watching all around him, feeling what the car and engine were telling him.

This was the day he'd waited years for and it was everything he'd hoped. Sure, he was a rookie, but within the first hour he discovered something important. He belonged here. Flying around the track, he knew he was doing what he was born to do. Maybe he didn't have the confidence or the years of experience of some of the guys, but he did have youth on his side, and a certain instinct that he didn't believe could be taught.

He took a couple of chances, but nothing crazy, moved up a few spots, absorbed the energy and excitement of the crowd even though he couldn't hear them, channeling the goodwill he knew was out there for a rookie.

And he found his zone.

The noise of the engines reverberated all around him, the heat built in the car, and the shifting kaleidoscope of colorful metal bullets flew by on all sides. And he was one of them.

Smoke ahead. No visibility. "Go high on turn three," his spotter said through the earpiece. He climbed, saw a space to squeeze between two cars and on his way out of the turn, took it.

"You're doing great. Hold it steady. Looking good on the straight." He felt a gut-deep excitement. What rookie didn't dream of winning or at least placing well on his first time out?

He could do it. He felt it in his bones.

And then his perfect day suddenly took a turn for the worse.

There was a noise he didn't like at all coming from the engine. Spluttery, and his speed wouldn't hold.

"What's wrong?" Stu asked.

"I gotta come in, something's wrong with the engine," he shouted into his mike.

He pitted, and in seconds the engine was exposed. Expert fingers poking delicately, like surgeons attempting to save a life.

"Probably a leaky valve," Stu told him. And Sawyer cursed the wasted time as they replaced the part.

Then he was off, having lost valuable time.

Within two laps he knew the problem wasn't solved.

Back to the pits.

Turned out to be a faulty fuel line. Which they replaced. More time lost.

He roared out, his blood pounding, feeling an insane urge to go like crazy and damn the consequences.

But the scarf was a soft patch over his heart. As he thought about Lucy and some of the things she'd said to him, he calmed down.

And realized something important. He wasn't going to win every race. It didn't mean he needed to act like a fool. All he could do was his best.

And the best was his responsibility…for the team who'd worked so hard to get him here, for the owners who'd taken a chance on a rookie, for the sponsors who were putting up good money to keep him driving. For his family, who were here to cheer him on.

For Lucy.

He didn't need to win a race for any of them, not today.

He needed to show them he was a man worthy of their trust.

I believe in you, she'd written.

You didn't let down a woman with that kind of faith.

So, he regathered his concentration. Put the bad luck out of his mind and drove as he'd never driven before.

He didn't win. Didn't place. Wasn't in the top ten. None of his fantasies of his first NASCAR Sprint Cup Series race came true.

He finished in the bottom quarter.

But as he pulled himself out of the car, he felt great.

"Sorry about the mechanical, man," Stu said, slapping him on the back.

"Stuff happens."

"How do you feel?"

He grinned. "I feel great." He gave Stu a bear hug. "We finished our first race. We did it."

Stu hammered him on the back with his fists. "You got it. And the next one will be better."

"I know."

LUCY'S FEELINGS WERE so mixed they could have been run through a blender.

She was proud of Sawyer for his performance, thrilled that he was taking an unspectacular first race in stride.

And sad that whatever magic he'd believed she had hadn't helped him.

Her gift last night had been spontaneous. Now she felt like a fool. Who gave a grown man a scarf she'd been wearing?

Clearly she'd spent too much time with gay men.

And then Sawyer was advancing upon her, the look in his eyes both tender and warm. Last night came rushing back to her and, running forward, she opened her arms before he got to her.

He kissed her long and deeply. His skin was hot, his cheeks stubbled and his uniform scratchy. She didn't care.

She pressed closer.

After he'd kissed her so long she thought he might have forgotten they weren't alone, he pulled back, still holding her close.

His face was so dear to her, she couldn't imagine not seeing it anymore, except on television. "Thank you."

"For what? You didn't come close to winning."

"Yeah," he said. "I did. I found a woman who believes in me. I love you, Lucy."

"Oh, Sawyer." She felt so overwhelmed she wanted to cry. Which was ridiculous. She never cried. "I have to go home tomorrow."

"Yeah. I know. Me, too."

"We live on opposite sides of the country."

He scooped a thumb under her lower lashes and caught a tear. "Yeah, I know."

She sniffed. "I'm crazy about you."

His smile was a big, goofy grin. "Yeah, I know."

"Do you think you could say something besides, 'Yeah, I know?'"

"I'm crazy about you, too. I can't figure out our whole future right this second, but we're going to have one. A long one, lasting approximately forever. We'll work it out."

She sighed in pure bliss. "Yeah," she said. "I know."

* * * * *

With thanks to Tom Sims for the fabulous
Daytona photographs, to my brother,
Jim Burch, for tales of Bequia,
and to Ken, for being the positive,
wonderful man that you are.
Happy Valentine's Day!

THIS TIME AROUND

Dorien Kelly

Dear Reader,

First, let me say how thrilled I am to be included in this anthology with Vicki and Nancy. They are amazing people and writers!

When I started this project, I was certain that I wanted my heroine, Megan Carter, to be a rookie NASCAR Sprint Cup Series driver. She has achieved an incredible feat but still has much more she can do. Very few of us have been in Megan's exact shoes, yet we're all working toward our goals. It can be scary putting ourselves out there and grabbing for our dreams, but the challenge adds spice to life!

Megan is striving to make herself faster and smarter with each race. She'll get there. She's also striving to learn to open her heart to love. Good thing she has met Chris Donahue, a man who not only knows who he wants to be his Valentine, but in the face of likely rejection will take a ferry to a puddle-jumper flight, and then two more plane rides to get to her side. While Chris and Megan are opposites on the surface, deep down—where it really counts—they're meant for each other.

May we never lose faith in ourselves...or in love. And if you should ever want a pep talk about just how fabulous and powerful we women are, drop me a line at dorien@dorienkelly.com or visit with me on Facebook or Myspace. And do check out my Web site at www.dorienkelly.com for info on my upcoming books!

Dorien

CHAPTER ONE

MEGAN CARTER DRIFTED from a delicious dream, one as warm as the Caribbean and as sensual as the knowing smile of a certain man she would never, ever forget. He was there, with her, in that dream… and she wanted to stay.

Just one more minute, she silently negotiated, not sure exactly who she was negotiating with, other than herself. All she knew for certain was that while she had dreams of Chris, she'd never have the real man again. She had intentionally eliminated that possibility when she'd sailed from the tiny windward island of Bequia late last month. It had been the right thing to do, both for her career and for her cautious heart.

But right seldom meant easy, so she clung to those dreams. And if she had to wake, couldn't it at least be to sounds more soothing than those of her twin brother, Stewart, banging around in her motor home's galley?

"Get it in gear, sis," Stewie called through the door to her sleeping quarters. "It's Tuesday of Speedweeks and you're the rookie they're all hot to see. You've got a bunch of television interviews in two hours."

Megan rolled onto her stomach and burrowed under her pillow, unwilling to give herself over to reality. Not that her current reality was horrible. Totally the opposite, in fact. After three years as a driver in the NASCAR Nationwide Series, she was thrilled to be with a new team, Hammond Racing, and finally competing in the NASCAR Sprint Cup Series.

Heck, she'd been working toward a NASCAR season opener in Daytona forever. Or at least since she'd been eight years old and a rookie competing in youth quad racing with Stewart. The teasing and resentment she'd taken from the boys for being— ick!—a girl had only fed into her need to win. And so she'd kicked some major butt and continued to do so until here she was, at Daytona, bringing her game up yet another level.

And because she'd known that this racing season was going to take more out of her than she had in energy reserves, in January, she'd given herself nearly three weeks cruising the Caribbean on a charter sailboat. Her only companions had been the couple who'd served as the small catamaran's crew. Megan had been content with the near solitude; she didn't get much of that in life. In fact, until they'd reached Bequia, she'd found little reason to leave the boat. Then everything had changed.

"Come on, Megs," Stewart called while rattling the door. "Vacation's totally over. Get moving."

Megan rolled onto her back, placed her palm against the delicate necklace with its gold coral charm that rested against her skin, and frowned at the linen-covered ceiling of her home away from home. Her brother was being a pain, but that was his job. He was also her fitness coach, chef and best friend, all rolled into one easygoing body. She wished she could be as mellow as Stewie, but she seemed to have inherited the full dose of the Carter Obsessive Gene. Nothing by half measures. Ever. And this morning, she was seriously obsessing on the man she'd left behind.

Actually, the longing thoughts had started the moment she'd climbed into that dinghy at the end of Chris's dock and departed from paradise. She had worked hard last week and this to hide her distracted state from Stewart and all the people whose jobs depended on her growing success—her crew chief, her team, her over-the-wall crew. But if Stewart, with his nudge about vacation being over, had noticed, she knew they all had. Not good.

Success took the whole team, and if she lacked focus, they would, too. She'd made her share of personal sacrifices to maintain that focus…virtually no time at home, the inevitable drifting off from friends who weren't part of her NASCAR life, and no real romantic relationship in ages. As for the romance, until very lately she hadn't cared. She'd never been any good at discerning those men who desired her from those who desired the perks that came with dating a celebrity.

"Come on, Megan! Up!" Stewart demanded.

"Okay…okay, I'm up," she called to her brother, then sat upright so she wouldn't be making a liar of herself.

"Strawberry, banana or mango smoothie?" Stewie responded.

Megan wrinkled her nose. "None of the above."

Her brother tended to pack her liquid breakfast so full of wheat germ, protein powder and other gritty stuff that no fruit could cloak it. She might as well cruise on over to the beach and chew on a mouthful of sand.

The beach…

Daytona Beach wasn't Bequia's sleepy Admiralty Bay, but she'd take it over Stewie's paradox of a smoothie. Without giving it another moment's thought, Megan slipped from bed and pulled her workout clothes from the drawers neatly built into the bed's base. If she exercised, maybe she'd get fully back in the game, and she needed to…*quickly.* Matt Hammond, her new boss, wasn't the sort to suffer fools or randomly hand out second chances.

This coming Thursday, she had exactly one shot at qualifying for Sunday's big race. The irony that race day was also Valentine's Day didn't escape her.

All the more reason she needed to leave behind even the dreams of Chris Donahue and focus on her future. Hammond demanded star power, and she'd deliver nothing less.

"No time for breakfast," she called to her brother. "Gotta run."

Not that he was paying attention. The high-pitched whir of the blender greeted her as she slipped from the bedroom and into the bathroom, careful never to look fully Stewart's way. If she did, her smoothie fate would be sealed. Minutes later, teeth brushed, dark brown hair—as always—in a ponytail, and running shoes tied, Megan made good on her escape.

"I'll be back soon," she said over her shoulder. But soon wasn't the issue. Being heart-whole was.

CHRIS DONAHUE HAD BEEN convinced a decade ago that the Hammond portion of his relatives deserved its own wretched circle in hell. When he'd left Florida to make a life on Bequia, he'd sworn he would never come back. Too many times he'd been disappointed or been called a disappointment. Too many Hammond lies and too many Hammond manipulations. Yet here he was, drinking his morning coffee on a Ponce Inlet luxury home's terrace, taking in the sand dunes and the Atlantic Ocean just steps away. This was an ironically peaceful setting for a guy about to throw himself back into a whole lot of familial intrigue he'd intentionally left behind.

Chris hit a speed dial number on his cell phone that might as well have had cobwebs on it for all that it got used. But with each new phone, he kept the number logged for Susan, his father's secretary, even if he used it only when news about the old man's health drifted across the Caribbean and necessitated a call. Granted, that had been happening more frequently, as even his harder-than-steel father was not immune to the effects of time. But these calls were as close as Chris had ever been to the man, and not quite as far away as he'd prefer to be.

Susan, who was all things prompt and efficient, answered Chris's call on the second ring.

"Matt Hammond's office," she announced.

"So you're still trying to beat the sun to work?" he asked.

"Chris? Is it really you?"

"Absolutely."

"Then you should be asleep. Or still working."

Susan, who had visited Paradis, his beachside restaurant on Bequia, knew that it took a helluva lot of behind-the-scenes work to consistently deliver that paradise to his customers.

"Actually, I'm on a business trip," he said.

The statement, while not wholly accurate, remained true, as he'd agreed to meet with a potential investor so long as he was going to be back in these parts. Good thing, too. If he weren't meeting with this vacation home's owner, he'd be out begging for a room during Speedweeks. And while he was a pretty damn lucky guy, he wasn't *that* lucky.

"Really? Business where?" Susan asked.

Chris leaned back in the thickly cushioned wicker chair and did the math. "About ten miles from the old man's Daytona office."

"You're kidding!"

"Amazing as it seems, no, and I've got a favor to ask." He paused a second to also ask himself one final time if he was crazy, and the answer came back the same: yup, crazy as a mad dog in the midday sun. No news there. "I need credentials for the race. The whole thing…a hot pass, the drivers' and owners' lot…everything."

"Why aren't you asking your father?" Susan inquired, but they both knew the question was more rhetorical than real.

"For all the same reasons I haven't spoken to him in the past ten years," he said in a level voice.

"What's going on, Chris?"

He'd heard this question from Susan before. The first time had been back when he'd been a hurt and angry seventeen-year-old kid lashing out because he'd been dumped with a father he'd never known existed. The second time had been later that summer, when his older half brothers were making his life hell, and no one but Susan had given a damn. And the last time had been when he'd refused to reconsider attending culinary school instead of an Ivy

League school and had been cut off penniless by Matt "my way or the highway" Hammond.

"Look, I don't want to go into it, but it's not about the old man," he said. "I met someone. Someone who matters enough that I'm back here."

"A girl, then," she said with certainty.

Chris laughed. "You're dead-on, as always. An incredible girl."

The Fates had to find it a real joke that he'd get wrapped up with Megan, of all people. After that last play for control on his father's part, Chris had walled Matt Hammond from his life…made his way on his own, and on his own terms. And now he was compelled to come full circle, back around to the track and the racing life he'd abandoned.

But how could he not return? A guy came across Megan's combination of laughter, energy and sexy sparkle maybe once in a lifetime. And when she'd entered his world, he'd recognized that. But then he'd let her race off, which was quite possibly the biggest mistake of his life, and he'd made some killers.

"I'm happy for you, Chris," Susan said. "But you're asking for a lot."

Yeah, right now he was a walking example of desperate times demanding desperate measures. He should have told Megan who his father was the second the subject of her work had popped up, but he hadn't. At first he'd been too surprised to say much of anything, though he had considered offering his condolences. Then, he'd decided to wait for the perfect moment, which never arose, since perfect moments tended to be pretty damn rare. Finally, she'd bolted. And so now Chris needed to find out if she missed him as much as he'd been missing her. Because if she felt even a tenth of what he did, he had a whole lot of mending—and explaining—on his schedule this week.

"I promise that if you get me the passes, I won't screw up things with my father worse than they already are," he said to Susan.

She snorted. "That's not a tough promise to keep."

"The next one's a little tougher." And it was critical to Chris. "Don't call him as soon as we hang up and tell him I'm around, okay?"

"Now you're really pushing it."

"I'm not asking you to be disloyal. I'd never do that. The avoidance is as much for him as for me," he said. There was documented proof that he made the old man as crazy as the old man made him. "I'm not going to put myself back in his range of fire unless I absolutely have to."

"You're both acting like fools," Susan replied.

She hesitated before speaking again, and Chris began to wonder if he was going to have to come up with a Plan B, not that Plan A had been all that well thought out.

"There's only one way I won't tell your father I'm doing this," she finally said.

He knew what was coming next, and he was prepared to deal.

"It can be on your schedule, your terms, but you have to promise me that you'll talk to him while you're here."

Bingo.

"The two of you need to come to some sort of peace," Susan added.

They had, just not the peace Susan had hoped for. But he adored this woman, who had been his sole ally for that long and miserable summer he'd been under his father's roof. He would never say anything to hurt her.

"Good enough," he replied. "You have my promise."

He'd talk to his father as late on Sunday as humanly possible.

"Fine," she said. "Everything you need will be waiting for you at the credentials office."

Chris let out a slow breath of relief. What he really needed wouldn't be in the office, but she'd sure be at the track.

MEGAN WASN'T ESPECIALLY into camera angles or makeup tricks. She knew that she lacked sex-goddess glamour from any vantage point, though she was in good shape and did have a lot of All-American wholesomeness. But it was pretty tough to have even that come through when they'd set her up for this particular trackside interview looking directly into the sun.

She knew she should have grabbed her sunglasses from the motor home before the media sessions had begun, but she'd stopped over in the garage area, started talking with her guys, and totally lost track of time. Now she was paying the price. Her blue eyes, always sensitive to sunlight, stung. She felt as though she was looking through a wavy sheet of glass at the world beyond. A small crowd had gathered to watch the interview take place, but Megan couldn't begin to guess the number of people out there. She half wondered if her current interviewer, Miranda Carlyle, had made this adjustment intentionally. Miranda's show, *Talking Track,* was growing in popularity. Miranda, however, wasn't very popular among the drivers. Beneath that flawless exterior lay the cold personality of a shark.

"How does it feel to be the new girl on the track?" Miranda asked.

Megan had heard that question countless times today. But because a soft breeze had just picked up, soothing her raw nerve endings and burning eyes, and because she was a pro, she gave Miranda the answer with as much enthusiasm this time as she had the first.

"I like new beginnings," she said. Actually, she didn't have much to compare them to, since her life had been a string of new beginnings. She and Stewart had been six years old when their mother died in a traffic accident. It had been a confusing and scary time, but their dad had stood strong. After that, her little family of three had moved frequently for her dad's job changes, and then to promote her career. "And I like knowing that I'll be out on the track with the best of the best. This rookie has a lot to learn, and I can't think of a better group to learn from."

Miranda nodded her approval. "Has your welcome been warm at Hammond Racing?" she asked as a follow-up.

"Absolutely," Megan fibbed. While most of the Hammond team had been welcoming, Matt Hammond had been very frosty. Megan knew that her new job was due more to Hammond's eldest son and protégé, Ted, than it was to Hammond's enthusiasm. And even Ted wasn't much into warm-and-fuzzies. "It's a top-notch organization, and I'm honored to be a part of it."

"How nice for you," Miranda purred. "Rumor has it that Matt Hammond can be formidable."

"Mister Hammond is a legend," Megan firmly replied. *Did this woman think she'd complain on camera?*

Miranda leaned closer, as though she could gain any measure of conversational intimacy in such a public setting.

"So, Megan, have these changes in your racing life had an impact on your private life?"

Megan knew where Carlyle was going—to what she considered the forbidden territory of romance—and she didn't like it. She never heard the male drivers take this kind of garbage directly to their faces.

"I have a new motor home this season," she replied. "Well, new to me, at least."

The interviewer's smile showed more sharp incisor than charm before she spoke. "That's wonderful, but I think our viewers are more interested in whether they'll see you with a man by your side this year?"

Megan seriously doubted the viewers cared. This was just an interviewer with an agenda, but whatever... She'd play this as she always had, with a bit of teasing cluelessness.

"I'm with my twin brother, Stewart, all the time."

"Ah, but you know what I'm really asking," Miranda said. "Is there a special man you're seeing?"

Megan refused to let Miranda know that this line of questioning was getting to her, both for its rudeness and because it had fixed Chris clearly in her mind's eye. But if she showed weakness, Miranda wouldn't let go until Megan was fully bled for information.

"I like you, Miranda," she fibbed. "But if and when there is someone special in my life, he and I will be the only ones to know. I believe in keeping my..." She trailed off as a cloud drifted over the sun,

briefly giving her a clearer view of her onlookers.
"My…"

No way.

Impossible.

She was very good at envisioning things, then
making them happen, but she wasn't so amazing
that she could make a man materialize. Especially
one she'd already made disappear.

"Your…?" Miranda prompted.

Megan looked her way. "My…ah…"

She cleared her throat even though it didn't really
need it, and while she did, she glanced at the spot
where one very vital-looking ghost of a man gone
from her life had just been standing, but he was
gone. And so she turned back to her interviewer.

"I like to keep my off-track life just that—
off-track."

But it seemed to have followed her home….

CHAPTER TWO

DAMN.

He hadn't wanted it or intended it to be like this, but Chris was ninety percent certain that Megan had just seen him. Oh, she'd recovered well enough and quickly picked up with whatever the television reporter had been asking her, but he'd felt that jolt of recognition and hot focus.

That same awareness had risen between them when she'd walked into his restaurant on Bequia. He'd never forget that moment...and didn't want to. But because he also didn't want to distract her from her upcoming interviews with the lurking line of media types, either, he backed from the edge of the crowd to which he'd been instinctively drawn and continued to get the lay of the track.

He'd been here once before, but it had been a lifetime ago. Back then, he'd been at the tail end of an entourage that had had as little to do with him as possible. He'd seethed only as an adolescent could, and done his best to ignore his surroundings. Now, as he looked around, Chris had to admit that the place intrigued him, probably because this was Megan's world. Even now, with the big race days off, it seemed that there were as many people milling about on the grounds as lived on his tiny island. He could see why it excited Megan to be a part of this. The price had been too high for him, though.

Chris arrived at the gate to the owners' and drivers' lot, showed his credentials to the guard, and was waved in. He stopped just long enough to ask the gatekeeper if he knew the general vicinity where Megan Carter's motor home was parked. As it turned out, though, he would have found it on his own. Catching a few rays in a lounge chair next to the motor home was Megan's brother, Stewart. Even if Megan hadn't shown Chris pictures of her twin, there was no mistaking the resemblance. Stewart had the same dark hair and strong set to his jaw.

Chris approached. "Stewart, right?"

The other man opened his eyes and shaded them from the sun with his hand. "Yeah. Do I know you?"

"No. I'm a…friend of Megan's."

He'd stumbled a little, trying to figure out what modifier to stick in front of that generic word, *friend*. He wasn't an old friend since they hadn't known each other long. He wasn't a good friend since they hadn't parted on very amicable terms. He had been an intimate friend, but that wasn't the kind of thing that a guy pointed out to a girl's brother.

Yeah. Friend.

Maybe.

And her brother wasn't exactly helping him out with his tough-ass glare, not that Chris blamed the guy. If he had a sister, he was pretty sure he'd be on guard if some tan, shaggy-haired, beach-bum-looking sort came sniffing around. But that didn't mean Chris planned to share his résumé. Enough people on the grounds of this track knew him by name—not to mention by tales of his hell-raising—even if no longer by face. He wanted to remain unnoticed for as long as possible.

"I met Megan while she was on vacation," Chris said. "I live down that way."

"And?"

"And I'm in the area and I thought I'd stop by."

Stewart waved one hand in the direction of the lot's gate. "Pretty big thing to pull off, stopping by here, what with the security and all."

Chris shrugged. "I know people."

"Guess so, since you have the right credentials."

"So do you mind if I wait here for Megan?"

"She know you're here?"

"Sort of."

"What do you mean, sort of?"

He was being grilled as surely as if he were skewered on the shiny, new stainless steel number nearby. "I ended up watching a couple of seconds of an interview she was doing, and I think she spotted me."

"Spotted you? That doesn't sound very friendly."

Stewart swung his legs over the side of the chair, then stood. He reached into his shorts pocket and pulled out a cell phone. Chris got the distinct sense that a call to security was about to take place. More info would have to be shared, whether he wanted to or not.

"All right, here's the deal," he said. "I live on Bequia, and your sister sailed into the bay where my restaurant is located. She planned just to have lunch, but because I asked her to, she stayed until she had to go back home."

"Even though she'd never met you before that afternoon? Not a chance. You sure as hell don't know Megan. She doesn't even date any more without three personal references and a background check."

Chris had the feeling that Stewart was only half joking, if that.

"You don't know the quality of my food," he said, figuring a lame quip was better than nothing at all.

Megan's brother glanced down at his phone's screen and began scrolling though numbers, clearly on his way to 1-800-Nab-the-Stalker.

Chris tried to quickly think of some intimately identifying feature of Megan's that wouldn't also have this guy ready to flatten his nose. He figured he could probably take Stewart, but that was no way to start what he hoped would be a long and friendly relationship. Finally, a diplomatic approach occurred to him. Odds of having it work weren't good, but they beat being dragged out of here.

"Did Megan come back wearing a necklace?" he asked.

Stewart hesitated.

With no way to go but forward, Chris forged on. "And didn't you maybe think this was a little weird since all she'll ever wear in the way of jewelry is a watch?"

"Yes, she has a new necklace, but what does that prove?" Stewart asked in a grudging voice, apparently not quite ready to back down, but at least willing to listen.

"Is it gold and shaped like a fan coral?"

Megan's brother nodded. "That would be the one. She always wears it now."

Which was the best damn news Chris had heard in a very long time. If she still wore the necklace, she hadn't entirely cut him from her life.

"I bought her that to remind her of when we snorkeled in the bay by Moonrise, on the other side of the island," he told Stewart.

Megan's brother pocketed the phone. "Okay, but you should know that she's never mentioned you, and Meg and I talk a lot."

Chris accepted the sting of those words. "I didn't think she had. She walked away from me and told me not to contact her…that it was just one of those vacation things. And before you say it, I know that's not Megan, either. Look, all I'm asking for is a chance to talk to her. I'd never hurt your sister in any way. If she tells me to leave, I will. But I don't think that's what she wants. So I'm asking…just give me a shot at this, okay?"

Chris stood calmly under Stewart's deliberative gaze.

"I'm not BS-ing you," he said, when the silence had stretched just long enough to be uncomfortable.

Finally, Stewart backed off, relaxing his stance and giving a rueful shake of his head. "You sure picked one hell of a weekend to show up."

"I know the timing's bad, but it's not going to get any better until NASCAR's mid-July break, and I couldn't hold off that long. I got here as soon as I could. It's busy at the restaurant, and I have customers who expect to see me." He didn't add that many of those customers were of the rock star and business tycoon variety, and thus not easily dismissed.

"Well, take a seat," Stewart said, gesturing at the lounge chair. "I'll go pull another one from the bus, there. I don't know when Meg's gonna be back, but I'm betting one way or another, it's going to be one good show when she is."

Just so long as it wasn't of the smack-down variety, Chris was all for that.

MEGAN HAD HALLUCINATED. There was no other possible explanation. In the two hours since she'd last seen the Chris look-alike, she'd been to Hammond Racing's garage area and the hauler, taking care of business, and then had even skulked about the other teams' areas, looking for the man. If he were here, she'd have seen him.

And if it *had* been Chris, he would have stuck around. Even though a panicky sort of fight-or-flight mode had made her less than polite when she'd left Paradis, she knew that Chris wouldn't respond in kind. Despite his dangerous-guy appearance, he was a gentleman through and through. He'd never appear, then disappear, and let her stress out like this.

More than a little annoyed with herself for chasing a shadow, Megan waved to the guard at the gate to the drivers' and owners' lot, and walked toward her motor home. The air was spicy with the scent of grilling food, and her stomach growled. After ducking Stewie's not-so-smoothie, she hadn't had the time to grab anything else. It was now midafternoon and she felt as though she could eat her own weight in whatever deliciousness was cooking on that unseen grill.

And the closer she came to her own motor home, the stronger the wonderful scent grew. Maybe Stewie had taken to swapping recipes with some of the other motor home drivers? A lot of them doubled as cooks for their employers, and many had restaurant experience.

Megan rounded the far side of her motor home, to the entry side, then stopped in her tracks. It seemed she had her own Michelin-rated chef.

Chris—and it *was* him, the sneak!—stood shoulder-to-shoulder with Stewart at the grill, their backs to her.

Megan tried to take stock of the situation and her emotions, but both were too tangled for her even to begin to unravel. Before she could decide what to say, Chris must have sensed her presence because he turned from the grill. Until this moment, she'd always liked that they were so attuned.

He took a step toward her.

"Hey," he said. "Sorry if I messed up that interview for you."

Her heart slammed an uncomfortable beat as anger mixed with the passion that rose every time she saw this man. "That's all you have to say? You're here…now…with no warning, and that's the best you can do?"

"It's not as though you've taken my phone calls or even answered the couple of e-mails I sent."

"What are you doing here?" she asked.

"Jerk chicken," said Stewart, who had turned to watch the action from his spot in front of the grill. "Killer recipe, too."

Megan ignored her brother. She hadn't gotten over finding him so buddy-buddy with Chris.

"I happened to be in the area on business, so I dropped in," Chris said. "I've been keeping your brother company."

She couldn't think straight. If she didn't want

him in her life, why did this offered-up-with-a-shrug answer annoy her? What did she want from the guy after she'd told him to go away? She had no idea. Life was so much simpler when not in...

Well, whatever it was, it wasn't love.

"Nice of you to stop by, then," she said, and then gave a pointed look at her watch. "I'm sure you have other places to be."

"I've made you angry."

"Yes... No!" She shook her head. "I don't know what I'm feeling."

"I could give it a good guess," he offered.

Stewart waved his tongs. "Think I'll get this chicken on a plate and take it inside. No point in letting good food go to waste."

Neither Megan nor Chris looked his way.

"So what do you think I'm feeling?" she asked.

"Shocked, angry, annoyed, but unless I miss my guess, also pretty happy to see me."

"You had me right until the end," she said. "I don't think happy's in the mix." Freaked out was, though, and in a big way, too.

He moved a step closer, near enough that she could catch the spicy scent that was distinctively Chris's. She'd been with him enough mornings that she knew he didn't bother with cologne or after-shave. This scent was just him—pure him. Megan shivered at the thought.

"Nice necklace," he said.

Instinctively, her hand went to where the necklace sat in the open collar of her Hammond Racing shirt. She'd tried to take the necklace off, and had even managed to tuck it away in a drawer for about twenty minutes, but she had missed it too much.

"I think it's pretty, that's all," she replied.

His smile said better than any words that he knew she was lying about its significance.

"Now do you want to know how I'm feeling?" he asked, but didn't give her a chance to reply. "I'm feeling tired after a ferry ride, a puddle-jumper of a plane and two longer flights yesterday. I'm feeling certifiably crazy for having done of all of this just because I missed a girl who was pretty damn plain that she never wanted to see me again. And I'll admit that I'm feeling just a little worried that you might have really meant what you said on the dinghy dock that morning."

So she wasn't an afterthought. It would have been so easy to tell him that she'd missed him, too. And it would have been the truth. But she'd made the right choice that morning on Bequia. Their lives were too different, so much so that they might as well live on different planets. Between her racing schedule and her sponsorship obligations, her life took place in a web of cities across the United States. His was focused on one little island, and she saw no reasonable space for compromise by either of them.

Much as she was thrilled to see him, she didn't

want to dive back into all of those feelings—hot, messy and glorious though they'd been. It would be the road to heartbreak, and she was determined not to let that happen.

The door to the motor home swung open and Stewart leaned out. "You guys want some of this chicken? It's the best damn thing I've ever eaten."

"No," they answered in unison, their gazes still locked on each other.

"All the more for me," Stewart said. The motor home's door closed behind him.

"What do you want from me?" she asked Chris.

"Your undivided attention, away from this place…these distractions."

But these *distractions,* as he'd put it, were her life.

He reached out and gently took the coral necklace between his fingertips. Megan's pulse jumped; her body wanted him even if her mind knew far, far better.

"Do you have any business obligations tonight?" he asked.

"No, nothing until morning," she replied almost involuntarily. She'd had dinner last night with one of her sponsors and had a meeting with both her agent and business manager tomorrow, and a party to attend on Thursday night after the qualifying race—her usual hectic schedule—but tonight was free.

He let the necklace settle back into place. "Then spend time with me."

Now that the physical link between them had been broken, she could at least think. "What would be the point?"

"Do you mean that?"

"I do." Or at least she meant something close to that.

He shook his head, then looked down at the ground before meeting her eyes again. "I've had this all wrong, haven't I? You meant it. I told your brother I'd leave if you wanted me to." He raised his hands from his sides. "And... Well, hell." He turned and walked away.

She told herself that this was the right choice... the safe choice...the reasonable choice. She might feel miserable now, but she'd feel better about it tomorrow. After she sobbed her heart out tonight.

He was a good twenty feet away before sanity kicked back in.

"Chris, wait!"

And when he turned to look at her, and his smile grew until they were both laughing, she knew that no matter what happened after today, she had made the *only* choice.

CHAPTER THREE

"HOW'D YOU LAND THIS PLACE?" Megan asked as they pulled up to a cheery, light blue-and-white shingle-style home that reminded her a little of the gingerbread houses on Bequia. Except those weren't large enough to house a small army, as this home was.

Chris glanced over as he put the rental car into park and turned off its engine. "It's owned by the man who wants to turn me into the next king of the television chefs or something."

She shook her head. "Somehow I can't see that."

"Me as a brand name? Nah. I'm more about the food and less about the publicity. I don't want my own Web site or cult of followers."

For a man with such talent—and killer looks that those TV chefs could only wish for—Chris possessed a surprising lack of ego. He scarcely noticed that women tended to gawk at him, and never had she seen him use those looks as leverage. She wondered how he'd managed to reach adulthood so unaffected. They'd never talked much about his family, except when he'd mentioned that his mom had passed away before his senior year of high school.

"Well, if you ever do want to go the media king route, I think you'll find it pretty easy," she said.

He laughed. "I'm too lazy for that stuff."

"Lazy? No way!"

He shrugged. "I am, in my own way. I'll stick with my island life. Still, it doesn't hurt to bat around a few ideas with a business expert—especially when it gets me a place to stay during Speedweeks. So, are you ready to go inside?"

Megan hesitated. "Is he here—the king-maker?"

Chris shook his head. "No, he's at his compound in Palm Beach. He'll be up this way tomorrow around noon to meet with me."

Suddenly, she was feeling a little uncomfortable about the implications of that overnight bag she'd agreed to pack.

"Then it's just us?" she asked.

Surprise and maybe a little hurt registered in his expression.

"Hey, it's me, Megan," he said. "You know I'll take you back to the track any time you want. All you have to do is say the word. And if you do decide to spend the night, there are at least six bedrooms in there that I've discovered so far. You can pick one with me in it…or not."

She sighed. She knew all of this and more. It hadn't been as though he'd been single-minded about getting her in bed the very day they'd met. She'd been the one making those impetuous moves.

"Sorry. I know I must sound like some sort of loon. I want to be here. But with all the stuff we've got hanging over us, I just don't know to what degree, if that makes any sense?"

"It does. And I'm not trying to make you uncomfortable. I thought we could use some private time in neutral territory. Your brother is great, but I didn't want him and everybody else around there watching us like we're some sort of reality-show episode."

She thought of her interview with Miranda Carlyle this morning. "That tends to happen in my line of work."

"I'd rather we got our act together—if that's where we're going—off-screen. Let's figure out what we are to each other—no pressure, sexual or otherwise. I mean, don't get me wrong, our lovemaking back on the island was phenomenal, but unless we both agree otherwise, this is a totally hands-off situation. Deal?"

He'd always understood her, even when she hadn't been so sure she'd understood herself. She wanted to think clearly, and not in the haze of amazing sex. Once that haze faded, she'd end up back where she'd been that last day in Bequia—confused and conflicted and ultimately, alone.

"Deal," she replied. "Hands off, all the way. I'd say let's shake on it, but we'd be messing with the pact before we even get out of the car."

He laughed as he pulled the key from the ignition. "We're going to be done in by our own deal, aren't we?"

"Time will tell," she said, then opened her car door.

Once out, she hesitated an instant, and then decided to retrieve her overnight bag, too. She could handle a night with Chris Donahue and not end up in his bed. A fine sentiment, not that she had any precedent to back it.

As they climbed the steps to the home's massive front door, she noticed that Chris was doing his best to hide a smile at the sight of that bag. She had to smile, too. Considering the whirlwind pace they'd taken their last time together, this new attempt at restraint was probably best defined as unnatural.

They entered the house, and Megan breathed in the mixed scents of the sea breeze and a slight citrus tang. To her nose, it smelled of wealth and luxury. And the place looked that way, too. Chris's potential investor either had very good taste or a very good decorator. The elegantly simple decor drew the crisp airiness of the dunes visible from the back window wall into the house, leaving Megan with a feeling of relaxed freedom much like she'd experienced at Chris's home. She set her overnight bag on a low-slung ivory leather chair.

"I think I can handle some time here," she said.

"Nice, isn't it? Hal and I are pretty much on the

same wavelength, which is the only reason I'm willing to talk to him about this idea of my branching out."

Megan, who'd grown up in a series of nondescript apartments and had a small but very nice home in Nashville that she hardly got to see, was just a little in awe of her surroundings. But more than that, she was curious.

"Mind if I snoop around?" she asked.

In his smile, she could see the never-back-down guy who'd challenged her in Bequia.

"Why not? I have," he said.

Chris showed her the tropical-themed formal dining room and a quiet and intimate library that under other circumstances she would have lingered in. Right now, too much energy hummed inside her, including the sexual heat that simmered every time she was near this man. That she would quell the very best she could. She suspected, though, that her best wouldn't be enough.

"And now for my favorite room…" he said.

Generally, Megan was a kitchen philistine. So long as there was takeout available, she didn't see the need for one. And without takeout, her repertoire was limited to one item: scrambled eggs. This room, however, just might be enough to convert her. With its island-rustic cabinetry in contrast to its top-of-the-line appliances, it managed to be big without being overbearing. And the fresh pineapple sitting in a wooden bowl on the granite countertop started her mouth watering.

"I can't believe I left that chicken with Stewart," she said. "I should have at least taken a leg for the road."

"Hungry?" Chris shook his head, then laughed. "I can't believe I asked that question. You're *always* hungry."

"Not very flattering, but true."

If not blessed with a speedy metabolism and a brother who pushed her exercise regime to the limit, Megan knew she'd be finding her vehicle's safety gear pretty tight.

"So you're going to feed me?" she asked.

Chris pulled open the door to the largest and fanciest-looking stainless steel fridge Megan had ever seen. He gave a low whistle, so she came behind him to see what could be more awe-inspiring than the exterior of the appliance.

"Hal wasn't kidding when he said he'd stock the place for me," Chris said over his shoulder.

Even Megan was impressed. In one quick glance she saw the distinctive orange label of her favorite champagne, plump strawberries and what looked to be a fluffy white coconut cake.

"Dessert is clearly covered," she said, ignoring the mental image of strawberries and Chris in a great big bed.

Chris, who was mining deeper into the stored

riches, replied, "That's not all. Want to put your appetite in my hands?"

She laughed. "That's dancing a little close to the hands-off restriction, but I'll risk it."

"Good deal. You won't be sorry." He pulled a plastic-wrap covered platter from the refrigerator. "Looks like Kobe beef. Nothing but the best."

"Which is your theory, right?"

"Yeah, but it's a little tougher to get the very best to an island of six thousand in the Grenadines," he said while placing the platter on the counter. "But every now and then, something amazing comes ashore. Life-changing, even."

Megan knew he was talking about her. The thought he'd apply words like *life-changing* left her equal parts flattered and scared. She wasn't ready to go there.

"I'm assuming you don't want any help in the kitchen?" she asked in a light voice.

Their gazes met, and she knew from the warm acceptance in his brown eyes that he understood what she sought.

Chris's growing smile was slow and sexy. "I'm going to be cooking outside, but I suppose you could do just what you did in Bequia?"

After one perilous joint luncheon preparation at his house, he'd told her they'd both be happier if he cooked alone. From that day on, she'd made it her goal to flirt him into distraction. She'd been pretty darned successful at luring him from the kitchen to the bedroom, too, but somehow the food had always turned out perfectly, anyway. Well, except for the time she'd incorporated a sensual dance into the flirting campaign. Just the memory of those days made her feel warmer.

"No repeat performance today," she said. "And never in the great outdoors with an audience walking the beach."

"You sure?" he asked.

"In your dreams, mister."

He laughed. "You've got that right. And vivid dreams they are."

He turned back to the refrigerator and began pulling out more ingredients. Megan pulled a stool from beneath the counter, sat and then enjoyed the view as he worked. Chris was tall from her vantage point of five-foot-five, and from any vantage point, well worth watching. Whether it was all the years he'd spent in the orchestrated chaos of a commercial kitchen, or a trait, he moved with a quick economy that was mesmerizing. And in Megan's opinion, incomparably sexy, too.

"Can you grab me the blue cheese?" he asked, distracting her from her ogling.

Megan walked to the refrigerator and opened it. "That would be...?"

He came to stand beside her. "The cheese that's looking a little blue." He retrieved it, then tossed it from hand to hand as he asked, "You really don't cook, do you?"

"Why, you didn't believe me?"

"I thought maybe it was a vacation ploy."

"No, that would have been when I pretended to be sound asleep each morning so you'd start the coffee."

"I figured that out the second day," he said as he returned to his cutting board. He gave her a smile. "I didn't care, either, since I kept you so busy playing."

They'd hiked and swum and snorkeled and sailed, and late one slightly rum-soaked night even had a sandcastle-building contest under the full moon. She'd loved every minute of it.

No matter how it looked on television or in the glossy magazines, being a driver could be a real grind, and Megan had started at it young. It had been her choice, and she held no regrets. But the same focus that now had her in the NASCAR Sprint Cup Series had also been a big, fat roadblock when it came to learning how to let go and have fun in other parts of her life. Until Chris.

He glanced up from his preparations. "I can feel you watching me."

"Just admiring the view." And thinking about a more unobstructed one.

He flashed her a grin. "You're easy."

He didn't know the half of it. Only with him, she was. And only with him did she want to be.

"You know, we might as well add a bottle of champagne to the meal," she said.

"Feeling festive?"

"Suddenly, yes." And in need of some play.

While he finished up the salad he'd been working on, Megan retrieved the champagne and placed it on the counter by the food, then found two crystal flutes in the cupboard above the small bar sink. She set those down and reached for the champagne at the exact same moment Chris did.

"That was a near miss in the hands-off category," she teased after their fingers had almost brushed. She held the bottle aloft. "But I came away victorious."

Chris laughed. "Gotta love a winner."

How she had missed this sort of intimacy.

"So do you know how to open that bottle in a nonrace-winning sort of way?" he asked. "I'd hate to see the contents go to waste."

"Easy," she replied while removing the bottle's foil and hood. "Nice angle, then you turn the bottle and not the cork. Like…this." The bottle released its cork with a slow hiss.

"Here," she said, holding the bottle out to him with her fingers splayed to cover as much surface as possible. "You pour."

"Then put the bottle down on the counter, champ. I see your game."

She couldn't help but smile back. "Where's your competitive spirit?"

"Alive and well."

Once she'd returned the bottle and its cork to the counter, he poured two glasses, then lifted one.

"For you," he said. He held it so that she had no possible way to accept it without touching him.

"Tease."

"There's no deying it," he replied while settling the glass in a more comfortable-looking grip. "We know you can dish it out, but how are you at taking it?"

"It all depends how it's served." Instead of bringing her hand to the glass's stem, she brought her lips to the rim. Their gazes met, and excitement bubbled inside her. Chris tilted the flute just enough that she had a sip of the dry and crisp beverage. And when she was done, she didn't back off. Winners never did. "When it's like this, I can take it just fine."

"I can't say I have any complaints, either."

His voice had carried a deeper timbre, one that reminded her of words whispered and secrets shared in a big bed with a ceiling fan lazily humming overhead.

"Want more?" he asked.

Much, much more.

Unsure of her own voice, she nodded. He fed her another sip, then put the glass aside.

"I don't recall the rules saying anything about mouths not touching," he said.

"Neither do I."

Time hovered between them, as present as their passion. Megan knew he could have taken the moment, stolen the kiss, but he didn't. Instead he lingered so closely that she could feel the heat of his body and hear his heartbeat. Or maybe she was hearing hers; her heart was pounding as quickly as it did in those instants just before the green flag dropped.

And when she couldn't take another second of anticipation, Megan brought her lips to his, claiming what she wanted. How she remembered this feel, this taste. It was as she'd dreamt this morning. Had it been that short a time ago? It didn't seem possible. This moment, though, she wanted to last forever.

She let her mouth teasingly dance across his, small nips of hunger, followed by a deeper kiss. And still, other than their lips, they didn't touch. These kinds of games she loved most of all—the ones in which they both could win.

Chris took up the challenge, as she knew he would. He brought the kiss even deeper, until she could think of nothing but him. Of being held by him. Of being loved by him. And then he broke off the kiss.

"You can't tell me you didn't miss this," he said.

She couldn't, so she stood silent. And hungry, though not for food.

He held out his hand to her. "What do you say?"

If she took what he offered, she'd soon be in his arms and then so tangled up in him that letting go would be nearly impossible. And if she didn't take it, she'd regret it forever.

"I've chosen a bed," she said, her voice trembling a little.

"You have?"

"Yes. The one with you in it."

And so he took her hand in his. Together, they stored the food, snagged the champagne, and let the moment lead where it would.

CHRIS WOKE SLOWLY, happily, and pretty damn worn out. They hadn't slept much last night. Between the talking, the love-making, the midnight meal they'd finally gotten around to when Megan had said she was too weak to go on, there had been little time left for sleep.

He liked the way she looked, sleeping beside him. Of course, he liked the way she looked in general—the curve of her lashes, the dimple that came out of hiding when she smiled, and the way her body fit so perfectly with his.

If he weren't so damn tired, he'd wake her and make love to her all over again.

And it *was* love.

For the first time in his life, he could think that and not have doubts creep in or find himself looking for some reason not to love her.

He got the geography issue and had to admit that it was going to take a lot of planning to work around it. But living in the comparatively remote area that he did, Chris considered himself the master of workarounds. Besides, he had enough cash saved from years of mellow living that he could afford a flight stateside every month and still not break a financial sweat. And if he partnered up with Hal, there would be more business-funded trips, too.

He could make this work. By sheer force of damn will, he could.

Chris shook his head when he let his mind still long enough to consider what he'd been thinking. Sheer force of damn will? He had more of his father in him than he cared to admit.

Megan stirred, and he reached a hand out to gently smooth her well-mussed hair from her face.

She smiled up at him, and in that instant he was thankful for that Hammond grit and willpower. He wouldn't be next to Megan without it.

"What time is it?" she murmured.

"Haven't looked. The sun's up, so it has to be after seven."

Megan shot bolt upright. *"Seven?"*

"Yes, seven. I take it you had plans?"

She scrambled from the bed, grabbing her robe as she did. "I need to have my morning run, then get to the garage and meet with Corbin—he's my crew chief—and then I need to call my agent, and I promised Stewart that I'd sit down with him and look at the updates he wants to make to my Web site." All of this had been delivered while she scooped up yesterday's clothes from the floor and then dumped them next to the overnight bag he'd carried upstairs a couple of hours ago.

"First, I'm not so sure that your morning run is a necessity," he said. "I can guarantee you burned some calories last night."

He'd thought she might smile, but all he got was a distracted nod.

"And you might consider one more thing before bolting off," he said as she dug through the bag, searching for anything at all to throw on.

"What?"

"A shower."

"Shower— Of course— Okay—" She dropped the clothes she'd been carrying and dredged out a black-and-white striped zippered bag.

He rose from the bed and headed to start the shower running for her.

"No way, mister," she said as he approached the bathroom door. "You get in that shower with me and we'll be delayed a few more hours."

"Relax, champ. I'd just planned to get it going, but thanks for the compliment. After last night, I'm not sure I have a few more hours left in me."

She blushed, and he was surprised she had that embarrassment left in her, considering the sheer—and wonderful—abandon she'd shown with him last night.

"Right," she said. "Sorry."

He laughed. "Now let me get the water started. By

the time you're done, I should have coffee ready. Want some breakfast, too?"

He thought of the breakfast he'd made her each morning in his kitchen: thick slices of mango and papaya, an egg-white omelet fat with fresh vegetables. She'd joked that she'd stop the world from spinning for that meal combination.

"No time," she said.

Apparently the world would keep spinning today.

He had just finished getting the shower set to her favorite too-hot-to-survive temperature when she appeared next to him.

"Sorry I'm being so frantic, but word has it the big man will be at the track every afternoon for the rest of the week. I need to be sure that everything is perfect in my corner of the world before he arrives today."

"The big man?" He had a damn good guess who that was. The past was coming up to kick him in the rear much faster than he had anticipated.

"Matt Hammond. He was supposed to be there yesterday afternoon while I was here, so if I don't get my face in front of him today, it's trouble."

"It can't be that bad," he said, trying to step out of the role of someone who knew firsthand just how bad it could be.

She gave a short laugh. "Yes, it can. And since my car's in a go-or-go-home situation for the qualifying race tomorrow, let's just say he has me under a little more scrutiny. There are a lot of us fighting for two possible slots on Sunday. I have to win one of them or I don't think I'll last the season."

Megan was right. He knew his father thrived on that sort of survival of the fittest stuff. At least, that was the only reason that Chris had ever been able to come up with for the way Hammond had pitted his older sons against him.

Chris knew he was going to have to get past all those dark memories for the sake of this woman. He'd been fooling himself, thinking he could put off the dad issue. He owed Megan the truth. And before he could give her that, he needed to deal with Matt Hammond.

The good news was that his father was a man of firmly entrenched routines. A turkey-breast sandwich on whole-wheat bread—no mayo—was the daily lunch he demanded. And mornings spent at Hammond Enterprises, the manufacturing company that had given him the wealth to step into NASCAR competition, was another unbreakable rule. Chris would go there this morning. He knew Susan would get him in to see the old man.

"Then let's start moving," he said to Megan. "Get in the shower. I'll go take one, too, and then we're out of here."

Megan smiled with obvious relief. "You're the best!"

But would she feel that way once he told her who his father was?

CHAPTER FOUR

"THANK YOU SO MUCH for doing this with me," Megan said as she led Chris toward the garage where Corbin and the rest of her crew were probably already hard at work.

Action started early during Speedweeks. Already, fans were milling about, and clusters of media people were grabbing what opportunities they could to snag drivers and crew chiefs. Megan had too much to get done this morning to accommodate the fans as much as she wished she could. She knew the media would find her whether or not she wanted them to.

"I really wanted you to see what I do, up close, and meet the people I work with," she said to Chris. "I promise I'll have you out of here by nine, with lots of time to get ready for your meeting with Hal of the amazing house."

"Amazing enough that I might be able to talk you into going back there tonight?" Chris asked.

"I don't know. Maybe. Depends on how things go today. And if I do go, we have to sleep at least a few hours, okay?"

"I'll do my best." He gave her a quick smile. "Or maybe that means I won't do my best. Just consider it, okay?"

She nodded, then stopped Chris and had them change their course when she saw a lone cameraman loping her way.

"You mentioned that Matt Hammond won't be around this morning," Chris said. "Who do you think I'll meet?"

"You're definitely going to see Corbin McCullough," she said. "He's been with Hammond Racing forever. I was a little worried about stepping in with him, but he's a nice man. He even smiles occasionally, unlike the Hammonds. I think it must be genetic."

"What must be?" Chris asked.

"The inability to smile."

"Hope not."

"So you're on the nurture side of the nature/nurture debate?" Megan asked, even though it had almost seemed as though he'd been talking to himself.

"Sure," he replied, now sounding a little distracted.

She slowed her pace now that the cameraman had headed off in another direction. "Is everything okay?"

"Sure," he said again.

"Okay," she replied, even though she had the distinct sense that whatever was going on in Chris's head wasn't even close to okay. About halfway to the garage, their path crossed Corbin's.

Megan called his name, waving him down.

The older man nodded a greeting and came her way. "I was just heading over to the hauler."

"We'll come along," Megan said. "And, Corbin, this is Chris Donahue. Chris, this is Corbin McCullough, who is, in my opinion, the best crew chief in NASCAR."

Chris gave a hello and held out his hand to shake the older man's. "Hello, Corbin."

Megan's crew chief took Chris's hand and shook it, but he had a quizzical expression on his face. Still, all he said in return was, "Chris."

Corbin was a man of few words, but not often one of odd looks. Generally, his weathered face showed about as much emotion as a professional poker player's. Short of cross-examining him, though, Megan would never know why he'd done a double take, so she dropped it.

As they walked, Corbin updated her on some adjustments they'd been making on her car, since it had been handling a little tight. Megan confirmed what she needed to, but had faith in the crew chief and the rest of the crew.

They arrived at the blue-and-yellow hauler splashed with the colorful logos of her top sponsors, and Megan said to Chris, "Come on in. I'll give you a tour."

"Sounds good," he said, but he still seemed off.

Her best guess was that he was withholding something from her, but that wasn't like Chris—or at least the Chris she was fairly certain she knew.

They climbed the stairs into the back of the hauler. She was a little surprised that Corbin didn't move on to the door to the war room at the front, choosing instead to stand next to Chris. She supposed there might be some novelty in seeing her explain a place he could navigate blindfolded and hobbled.

"Right now, there's not much in here except for our spare parts inventory, but it's a tight fit when the car and all the tool boxes are in place," she said to Chris. "It's amazing the way it's rigged, though. Everything has a designated spot, just like a giant jigsaw puzzle."

"I'd imagine it takes a lot of money and engineering to put one of these together," he said.

"It does," she said. "Corbin, do you know off the top of your head how much it costs to rig out a hauler?"

But Corbin didn't answer. He just kept looking at Chris, who seemed to be pretending Corbin wasn't there at all. Megan resigned herself to ignoring the strangeness for now.

"Well, it's a lot," she said in a perky tour-guide voice. "All the more reason I want to make a good showing this weekend. A few more endorsements would help me sleep better at night." She pointed upward, to where a car identical to hers waited on a hydraulic ramp. "That's my backup car. Let's hope I don't need it."

"You won't," Corbin said.

He turned his attention to Chris. "Good to see you."

And with that, he was out of the hauler and gone.

"That goes up to the top of my close encounters of the strange kind list," Megan said to Chris. "What did he mean by 'good to see you'?"

Chris shrugged casually enough. "That it was good to see me?"

"Have you seen him before?"

"I suppose he could have come into the restaurant at one point or another."

"Then he would have mentioned it, don't you think?" Megan asked. "And it's even weirder yet that he left before doing whatever he came here to do."

"Maybe he's running late." Chris looked at his watch. "And we'd better get moving if you're going to show me around before I have to get out of here."

Okay, then. They'd been on the track's grounds for less than half an hour. She wondered if she wasn't getting what her dad called the bum's rush, back when he'd first been seeking endorsements for her. Sure felt like it.

"Come on up this way to the war room," she said as she led the way. "It's our office on wheels, where we can review tapes of races and have meetings without being right up on top of media or the other teams." She reached for the door. "And best yet, it's air-conditioned. I can't tell you how much I like that."

She swung open the door, and a group of people obviously in deep discussion turned and looked at her. Her stomach clenched when she realized that one of them was Matt Hammond. With his steel-gray eyes, deeply tanned skin, and military-style brush cut almost exactly the same color as those chilly eyes, he was never the most approachable of men. And now he looked as though he'd hurl a thunderbolt in her direction if he had one handy.

"Sorry to interrupt," she said to the group, then added a "Good morning, Matt."

Everybody but Hammond murmured a greeting in return. He just kept working on that Zeus-like stare of wrath. Megan quickly considered what she might have done to offend him, except walk in here, which hardly seemed to merit a death sentence. She came up blank. Except she now realized that Matt wasn't looking at her at all.

"How did you get in here?" he asked Chris, who'd been just a step behind her.

Chris moved to stand next to her, but before he could speak, she said, "He's with me."

Hammond ignored her.

"Step outside," he ordered Chris.

"Look, I'm sorry," Megan said in an effort to smooth over whatever the heck was going on. "I didn't know you would be having a meeting this early, and—"

Chris lightly touched her elbow. "It's okay, Megan."

Hammond was heading their way.

"Outside," he said again.

Instinctively, Megan turned.

"Just him," her boss said. "You wait here."

Matt Hammond had always been tough and frosty, but he'd never been so close to rude with her. Megan felt her temper beginning to rise.

"He's my guest and I'll see him out of here, if that's okay with you," she said. She'd managed to pull out some politeness, but she'd encased the words in the same steel he used.

"Do you want to be the driver of the 341 car to-morrow?" he asked her.

"Of course I do."

"Then stay where you are."

She looked over at Chris, but he was locked into some sort of stare-down with Hammond that she didn't understand.

"After you," he said to the older man. Then he flashed her a smile. "See you in a few."

Megan wasn't so sure.

CHRIS FOLLOWED HIS FATHER out of the hauler, wryly noting the older man's ramrod-straight posture. He might be older, thinner, and grayer, but Matt Hammond in all other ways remained the rigid man of Chris's youth.

About five yards from the hauler, Chris's father stopped dead and turned to face him. "How did you get your credentials?"

Luckily, Chris hadn't been expecting a "how have you been?" or other social nicety.

"Susan gave them to me in exchange for my promise that I'd look you up and talk with you," he replied.

"That was outside her authority."

"If you're looking for a bad guy, look here."

His father's twitch of a smile held no humor. "Same place as always, isn't it?"

"Time to let it go, Matt."

The moment his father's given name escaped his mouth, Chris regretted the move. Nothing enraged Matt Hammond more than a perceived act of disrespect. And while his father's words had cut, Chris had known that the passing years wouldn't have altered his father's opinion of him. He had been tried and convicted for crimes against the family, and that would never change.

"Leave."

"I will, for today, and only after I've seen Megan."

"Not an option." His father had forced the words through his teeth as though he'd been taking diction lessons from Clint Eastwood. "I said, leave."

Chris had gone over a decade without direct paternal contact. All in all, it had been a good decade, too. Surely he could balance that against this one short encounter and hold on to his patience.

"I'm not a criminal. I'm not a spy. I am no risk to your team or driver," he calmly replied. "And I will talk to Megan before I leave to get my business done for the day. I suppose you could have me dragged out of here, right now, but that's going to be bad press." He hitched his thumb toward a small cluster of curious onlookers. "People are already wondering what has you so ticked off."

Matt Hammond never backed down, but he did turn his back on people. Not for the first time, he did it to Chris. And not for the first time, it hurt.

"CHRIS IS INSIDE," Stewart said to Megan as she approached her motor home about fifteen minutes later. "Want to tell me what happened?"

"What didn't?" was the only reply she could collect herself enough to give.

She appreciated Stewie's obvious concern, but she needed to get all the facts, not just the cold lecture and ultimatum that Matt Hammond had given her through gritted teeth. And then maybe she could cool down. She'd kept her temper in check, but she hadn't buckled under Hammond's commands. He wrote her paycheck; he did not rule her life. She remained responsible for her own decisions, and she would make this one only after having heard Chris's side of the tale.

Before stepping inside, she gave her brother as reassuring a smile as she could. "Don't worry. I'll be okay. Just give me a few minutes with Chris and I'll be back out."

Stewart nodded. "Take your time."

Chris was seated on the sofa, looking as ragged as she felt. He stood as she closed the door.

She clasped her hands behind her neck and tipped back her head, trying to work out some of the tension that had settled right there. It was a lost cause.

"Megan…"

She shook her head. "Give me a second before we start this, okay?"

Chris returned to the sofa. "Come sit by me."

"Can't. Too much nervous energy." She paced a few steps past Chris and into the galley, where she opened the small refrigerator, then asked herself why she was even doing that. She closed it and turned back to face Chris.

"After he came back into the hauler, Matt Hammond spent more words on me than he has since the day I came on board," she said. "Among other things, he told me that you're not welcome anywhere near anything even remotely related to Hammond Racing. He told me that you take pleasure out of destroying things and lives. And he said if that I'm looking for a long career with his team, I won't welcome you into my life. Matt's a tough man, but he's usually fair. I don't know what you did to him, or when it happened…"

She trailed off as another thought occurred. She had some idea where it happened, at least. "So Corbin knows you in the context of racing?"

"Not exactly."

"Then, how, exactly?"

He stretched his arms across the back of the sofa and stared up at the ceiling, appearing more drained than she'd ever seen him.

"Chris?"

He looked back at her, his brown eyes somber. Megan braced herself as though she was about to make contact with something solid and dangerous.

"Matt Hammond is my father."

"Your *father?*"

He shook his head as though he couldn't believe it, either. "The whole time I was growing up, I was told that my dad was a fireman who'd died trying to save people when I was just a baby. They all lied. Days after my mom passed away, my aunt told me the truth."

Megan tried to concentrate on what Chris was saying, but all she could focus on was the past. She could almost feel the excitement and pride she'd glowed with while telling him about joining Hammond Racing.

"I told you when we first met who I worked for," she said. "Don't you think that then might have been a good time to have mentioned something like, 'Hey, that guy's my dad'?"

"Megan, I know this is a mess, and that I could have handled it differently."

"*Differently?* Take everything you've done and turn it a one-eighty. That's how differently you could have handled it."

"I was going to see him at his office today. I needed to get some things nailed down before I talked to you, but I was going to tell you."

"Easy to say now," she said. "And pardon me if I have a hard time believing you'd get past the receptionist."

And then it all came clear. "You used me. Everything we had down on the island was a lie. You were using me to get to your father."

He rose. "Okay, you're upset, so I've been trying to cut you some slack, but if you think that I've just been working you to get to my father, you've crossed the line."

At this point, she flat-out didn't care.

"We'll put aside what that means you must think about my character, and whatever self-esteem issue you've got simmering over there, and just focus on the facts," he said. "I've spent eight whole weeks of my life with Matt Hammond and his sons, and let me tell you, they weren't weeks that I'd cross a street, let alone stoop so low as to seduce a woman, in order to repeat."

"What's that old saying…actions speak louder than words? Why the lies, Chris?"

"I never lied. I just didn't share everything."

"Nice. A liar's favorite defense for lying." She turned away from him to wipe away the angry tears she could feel collecting in her eyes. When she turned back, she said, "I can't believe I thought you cared about me."

"And I can't believe you think I *don't*." He started to say something, then stopped. "I'm leaving before I say something I'll regret."

Once he was gone, Megan let the tears fall.

CHAPTER FIVE

JUST WHEN A GUY THOUGHT there could be no more, there was. Chris had barely exited Megan's lot when he got collared by two autograph seekers, who, after snapping his picture, wanted to know who he was. He assured them that he was no one special. He didn't share that currently he fell more on the side of stomped-on and really ticked off.

"Chris!"

Instinctively, Chris looked to see who was calling his name, then damned his instincts. Ted, the elder of his two half brothers, was heading his way. All Chris wanted was off the track grounds and back to the relatively calmer world of restaurants, which was a damn scary comparison to be contemplating. Chris kept his head down and ignored Ted the Terrible.

"Hold up!" Ted demanded, following hard on his heels. "I heard from Corbin that you were here. We need to talk."

"Last time we did, it didn't go so well," Chris said.

Actually, even though Ted had been bigger and

eight years older, Chris had ended up flattening
Ted's nose. Bummer for Ted, because he'd pretty
much been the recipient of a flattening by proxy.
Chris had really wanted to nail Kurt, the other half
of the Hammond brothers' tag team of lies, sabotage,
and general crap-giving. But like all good bullies,
Kurt had fled. Thinking of either of them and what
they'd done to him made Chris wish for those days
of freewheeling fist-throwing. But he was no longer
seventeen and doubted he could stay out from under
the long shadow of the law if he decked Ted again.

Ted reached out and grabbed the back of Chris's
shirt.

"Bad move," Chris said while wrenching free.

"Wouldn't be my first," Ted replied.

To hear one of Matt Hammond's older sons admit
a flaw was akin to finding out that pigs really did fly.

Ted stood, palms out, in a position of surrender.
Another first.

"What do you want?" Chris asked.

"I want to talk to you about my…our…father."

"Probably not a good topic at the moment."

"You should know that despite appearances, he's
not doing well."

"I'm sorry to hear that." Which was the truth.
Otherwise, Chris never would have made those calls
from the Caribbean.

Ted nodded. "Thanks. I know you don't have
much reason to like him."

"Most of which is your doing. Well, yours and Kurt's." He paused, then asked, "Where is Kurt?"

"Kurt's not part of the company anymore."

Even though Kurt was younger than Ted, he'd been the alpha dog and heir apparent the last time Chris had been around them.

"Why?" he asked.

"A poor choice of wife, in Dad's eyes. Either the wedding had to be canceled or Kurt was out. The wedding took place, and Kurt is working in open-wheel racing."

"Interesting games of brinksmanship you guys still play."

Ted shrugged. "I mostly avoid the games these days. They're too time-consuming when there's real work to be done."

He'd taken the moral high road for efficiency's sake? Very Hammond-like, Chris thought.

"So, other than telling me that Matt's not doing well, what do you want?" he asked aloud.

"I want to ask you to stay away from Megan Carter the rest of this week."

Chris shook his head. "You're not as far out of that brinksmanship league as you think. Problem is, you have no leverage on me. What are you going to do, start another game of 'Blame Chris'? I don't give a damn what Matt thinks of me."

"I'm asking you this—"

"Whatever you do, don't say brother-to-brother."

Chris saw a little of himself in Ted's quick smile. "Wouldn't dream of it," his half brother said. "I'm asking you this for Megan. Apparently, you two have something going on."

"You could say that." He would have been hard-pressed to define what that "something" was at the moment.

"I fought hard to get her into Hammond Racing, but just because she's in the door doesn't give her any measure of safety."

"As I well recall," Chris said.

Ted gave an impatient shake of his head. "We can hash out that stuff later. I'll even let you take another swing at me if it means you'll listen now."

"Sounds like a fair deal. Go on." He'd wait till the end of the week to decide whether he'd really take his half brother up on the offer.

"Megan needs to qualify tomorrow and do well on Sunday, or Dad will have her out of here just as fast as she came in. I don't want that. A couple of seasons under her belt, and I'm convinced she'll be a champion. She's good, Chris. *Really* good. She's smart and motivated, and—"

"You don't have to sell me on her."

"No, but I do have to sell our father. If you distract her, and she underperforms, I don't think I have the sway to rescue her. I'm still in the doghouse for the driver Megan replaced."

"And so what you're telling me is that I need to stay away from Megan for her own good?"

"Yes."

Chris laughed. "Don't ever say something that chauvinistic to her face or she'll make sure you're getting your nose fixed all over again. I'm not going to back off to *protect* her. She knows what position she's in, and she's damn capable of protecting herself. Let her decide."

Ted scowled, looking every inch his father's son. "Hey, I asked, and if anything bad happens, it's at your door."

"Whether it's my fault or not. Nothing new there, either. See you around the track, Ted," Chris replied, and then pulled a Hammond move of his own, striding off to leave Ted in his wake.

Like father, like son.

Just not too much alike, Chris hoped.

MEGAN WOKE THURSDAY morning, suffering from what she could only peg as an emotional hangover. She lay in bed, trying to block out both the sounds of Stewie banging around in the galley and thoughts of what Chris might be doing right now.

She'd slept well last night, but only because around ten, Stewart had wisely given her a rum and diet tonic to drink as she'd talked herself out. By the time she'd finished dumping her woes on her brother, she'd felt drained but not recovered.

Whether Stewart had recovered from the verbal hiding she'd given him when he'd tried to explain how guys think, and why what Chris did made perfectly good sense to another guy, she wasn't certain.

"Strawberry or mango?" her brother called good-naturedly.

Apparently she hadn't wounded him for life.

"Mango, hold the beach sand," she called back, and he laughed.

As she stretched and steeled herself to get on with her day—the biggest yet of her career—her cell phone rang. She plucked it from its perch on the nightstand built into the wall and looked at the caller ID.

Chris.

Megan hesitated, but knew if she didn't answer, she'd just obsess later. And so she hit the talk button.

"Hello?"

"Good morning," he said. "I just wanted to call and wish you good luck this afternoon. What time does the race start?"

"Two-thirty," she replied.

"I'll be thinking of you."

She held the phone a little tighter. She had so many questions, so much to say, but now was not the time. Not when sixty laps would soon determine her fate.

"Thank you," she said.

"You're welcome, champ. You can do it," he replied, then said goodbye.

Sixty laps.

When they were done, she would think of Chris.

"READY TO ROCK AND ROLL?"

Corbin's voice came though Megan's helmet loud and clear. She shifted in her seat a little, making sure she was in that sweet spot where everything was just where it should be in front of her...not even a millimeter off.

"More than ready."

And she knew she needed to be. Twenty-eight drivers all shared the same goal: to be first across that finish line.

Megan allowed herself to take in her surroundings—the heat of the day, the heat of the moment, the noise, the excitement, the absolute hunger to win. *This* was what she lived for. And as she took her starting position, Megan thought the same thing she did before the drop of each green flag: *This time around, I'll do it better, faster, smarter.*

She and Corbin had talked a lot this morning. They agreed that with the hot, sunny day and its effect on track conditions, if no one got tangled up in the first dozen laps, the race was going to string out. She needed to come out hard and get to the front. There'd be no gaining position without a whole lot of struggle later in the race. If she drove smart and clean, she'd be fine. And if fate threw a few bones her way, she'd be racing on Sunday.

Better...
Faster...
Smarter...

The green flag dropped, and Megan's world narrowed down to an oval track and twenty-eight hardened competitors.

CHRIS HAD HAD EVERY intention of staying at Hal's house during the race. Megan needed her space, and the duo of Hammonds he'd ticked off needed a day to cool down. The game plan had been to finish dissecting Hal's written proposal for opening a signature restaurant in Miami, then take a run to the nearby lighthouse. He'd stuck with the plan until about two o'clock, then admitted to himself that the only place he wanted to be was at the track, watching Megan.

He'd fought his way through traffic, then given his patience the workout it needed while parking and getting through the admission gate. The race was on lap twenty by the time he'd gotten into the stands. According to the couple next to him, Megan had moved up through the pack quickly to settle in the sixth spot and was holding tight to her position.

As Chris watched, he grew accustomed to the rhythm of the race, but he never wholly relaxed. Not with Megan out there. Something that had once been exciting but impersonal was now very personal. The woman he loved was out there in that pack of machines. He moved forward in his seat, fascinated when the car behind her tried to make a move, and she came just far enough off the inside to hold him back.

Chris had accused his brother of brinksmanship, but this was brinksmanship brought to the level of art: one big dance of steel and rubber and cast-iron nerves. And Megan looked to be every bit as good at it as Ted had claimed. She was made for this sport.

On lap forty-five, the two lead cars, which had been trading positions, locked into an epic struggle high on a turn. Chris held his breath as the second car spun, then righted itself. The front part of the pack, including Megan, maneuvered past it in moves so seamless that he found himself on his feet. Megan even managed to take one more car, muscling her way into the fourth spot.

"How many laps left?" he asked his neighbors.

"Fifteen."

He wanted this for her more than he'd thought possible. He couldn't give her the world, but he would cheer her on as she made it her own. Chris held his breath as the car she'd passed just moments ago reasserted itself and moved her back to fifth.

"It's okay," he said as though she could hear him. "It's all good."

From what he understood, she had to be in the top two of the cars that hadn't otherwise already qualified to race on Sunday—the go-or-go-home cars.

He wished like hell he knew whether anyone in front of her was go-or-go-home, but he didn't. The best he could do was figure the odds with only four cars in front of her and hope they didn't let her down. She'd had enough letdowns already, including those from him. And he would work as hard as she was doing right now to be sure he'd never again be a source of sorrow in her life.

MEGAN LET OUT A WHOOP of joy when she crossed the finish line. Better, faster, smarter…she'd done it all!

"Nice work," Corbin said in his typical understated fashion.

"Thanks," she replied through her helmet mike, trying for his level of cool. Impossible, of course, when she'd just been howling as though under a full moon.

Time flew as she turned the No. 341 car over to the crew, did a quick race review with Corbin, and then headed toward the hauler, where she'd been told that Matt Hammond was waiting to congratulate her. After that, she planned an endless shower and a nap before she dressed for the sponsor party she had that night.

"Megan!"

Megan held back a groan of impatience. Miranda Carlyle was heading her way, with her cameraman dog-trotting behind her.

"Just a quick interview," the reporter promised, following her words with a baring of teeth bleached so white that they looked like plastic.

She nodded her assent, though all she wanted to do was keep moving.

"Megan, you took fifth place, and first among the go-or-go-homers. You must be surprised to find yourself in the big race on Sunday," the reporter said once the camera was in position.

Nice little barb in that statement, Megan thought.

"I'm not so much surprised as pleased. We worked hard and executed well. I'm looking forward to Sunday's race."

"Any big celebration plans?" Miranda asked.

"I did my job, nothing more," Megan replied, ignoring the personal undertones of Miranda's question. "I'll save the celebrating until Sunday."

"And I'm sure you'll share with our viewers, then," Miranda said.

"About the race, yes. As for the rest of what you're asking me, not on a bet. Quit provoking me, Miranda," she answered flatly, then walked away.

Miranda's editors could cut that last bit and she'd still look golden, but the message had been delivered, and Megan felt all the better for it.

"Good job, champ," someone very familiar said a few moments later.

Megan's heart skipped with both a small thrill and a measure of nerves at the sound of Chris's voice.

"You mean, the race or giving it back to Miranda Carlyle?"

"That reporter back there?" Chris asked.

"Yes. She's a shark in tart's clothing," she said as he fell in step next to her.

He laughed. "In that case, both, but mostly the race. You were incredible."

"Thank you. It was one of those dream races. Everything happened just the way that Corbin and I anticipated," she replied.

"Planning is one thing, but execution is another. I watched you, Megan, and you blew me away."

"Well, thanks, but I can't do it alone. It takes my whole crew."

"Agreed," he said. "And it's no different in my business. But remember, they can't do it without you, either." He was silent for a moment. "I'd like some time to talk to you about everything that happened yesterday morning. We both said some pretty harsh things."

She nodded. "I know."

"I'd never use you, Megan."

She slowed her pace. "I know. I knew that last night, too. At least, I did in my head, if not my heart. I was so floored that you'd lie to me that all I could do was let the emotions out."

"I'm sorry. I can promise you that I won't hide anything from you again."

She gave him an appraising look. "I can't imagine

after the Matt Hammond Is My Dad bombshell, you'd have much more to hide."

He chuckled. "Other than a secret love of Chicago-style hot dogs, nope."

She laughed. "That, I can live with."

They had reached the hauler. Matt was up top on the viewing stand with Ted, and Ted's wife, Lisa. At least both Matt and Ted looked to be in good moods—as they should have been.

"Look, I have to go up and talk to Matt…um, your dad—"

Wow, this was awkward.

"Matt would cover it," Chris said.

"Okay, Matt, then. Anyway, when I'm done, maybe we could talk some more? I'm just not up for another Battle of the Hammonds right now, so if you could just head to my…"

She trailed off. Matt was coming down from the viewing stand. She must have used up all of her good timing on the track this afternoon.

"Hang on a second," she said to Chris, and hurried ahead of him without waiting for an answer.

Matt was two steps from the ground, but stopped when he saw her. Ted and Lisa were bottlenecked behind him.

"Well done, Megan," he said. "Corbin says you're in twenty-ninth position for Sunday's race. Not the best spot, but I'm pleased you made the cut."

Thank you, your highness, she wanted to say, but

didn't. That would have been just as rude as the imperiousness he'd shown yesterday...and in truth, right now, too.

"Thank you, Matt," she said aloud. "It was a great team effort."

"It didn't go unremarked."

Another thank-you was all she could come up with in response to that, after which a brief and awkward silence fell. In time, she was sure she'd become accustomed to dealing with Matt. Until then, she was content to survive each encounter.

"Is he with you?" Matt asked in a far less benevolent tone.

Megan didn't have to follow his line of vision; she knew he'd spotted Chris.

"Yes. We bumped into each other after the race," she replied.

"I thought I made it clear that he is persona non grata around Hammond Racing."

Okay, he was beginning to get under her skin. She'd just pulled off an amazing feat and all she could expect was a lukewarm atta-girl followed by a lecture? There was a limit to what one still slightly wound-up driver could take.

"We'll be out of here soon," she said in her sweetest voice. "I was just giving Chris the details for the Starworth Farms party he'll be attending with me tonight." Starworth Farms was one of her bigger sponsors. "Leona Starworth asked Chris to attend.

She's a big fan of his, after visiting Paradis last year." Lie. Total lie, but it added just the right twist to her statement. While Matt might be able to impose his will on her, no one pushed around Leona Starworth.

Matt looked as though he'd swallowed something sour. "I see."

She'd trumped him, and managed to do it without making it a direct power struggle.

"Well, thank you for the congratulations," she said. "And thank you for giving me this opportunity. Ted, Lisa, we'll see you at the party?"

"Yes," Ted replied at the very same time his father was saying no.

Megan wondered how it felt to be almost forty and under a father's thumb. She loved her dad, but was darned glad that he'd decided to return to Nashville when she'd turned twenty-one and let her manage her own career. He'd given up enough of his life for her dreams, anyway. She was glad to see him happy, remarried and chasing his own goals.

"Well, see you...or not," she said, then turned back to Chris, who was looking at her in a way that made her tingle down to her toes.

"We'd better get while the getting's good," she said when she'd reached him.

"So, champ, I'm going to a party tonight?" he asked once they'd cleared the other Hammonds.

Granted, his smile was contagious, but she wasn't yet ready to go down for the count. "You were handy ammunition, but that doesn't mean we're through talking about your Matt Hammond memory lapse."

Chris nodded. "I would expect no less."

"And I'm expecting a whole lot more," Megan replied.

The question was whether Chris could deliver.

CHAPTER SIX

WHILE A MOTOR HOME was sensible and functional, and Megan's might even be considered borderline posh, it was no place to try to dress for a dinner party. She looked at as much of herself as she could in the three-quarter-length mirror next to the shower. The dress worked, for sure. Its cerulean blue silk was cut just low enough to be a little flirtatious, but not so low that she was a paparazzo's dream. And just as the saleswoman had promised, it really brought out her eyes.

The red stilettos were a little tall, but she'd risk it; she liked what they did for her legs. Besides, without them her red clutch bag would look like a mistake. She wasn't too sure about the makeup. The light in the bathroom wasn't great, so she'd have to hope she hadn't clowned herself up.

"Are you ever coming out of there?" Stewart called. "I've run out of your embarrassing childhood stories to share with Chris."

Megan laughed. "Then start on some of your own. That should be good for another couple of days."

When she stepped out of the bathroom a few seconds later, both men, who were seated in the dinette area, stopped talking.

"What?" she asked as they stared at her. "Too much?"

"No," Chris said. "Absolutely perfect." He stood. "Are you ready?"

She moved toward the door, hanging her purse over her shoulder by its slender gold chain. "Yes, but the second I can get away with it, my shoes come off."

Chris's smile was intimate. "Just like on Moonrise beach," he said, out of Stewart's hearing.

More than her shoes had come off that night.

Tonight she swore she'd be stopping at the stilettos.

CHRIS PULLED UP TO THE country club where the Starworth Farms party was being held. As the valet approached to take the car, he glanced over at Megan, who'd been chatty, but only in a very superficial way, since he'd picked her up.

She'd made it clear that he'd been invited only because Matt, bless him, had annoyed her, and that this was his last shot at setting things right with her. He'd never regret their night at Ponce Inlet, but it had happened at the expense of finding time for true understanding. He was scheduled into meetings with Hal and his associates all day tomorrow and tomorrow night. And as Speedweeks continued to ramp up, Megan was going to have little time for him.

Tonight was the night.

The valet jogged up and opened Megan's door. She exited the car as gracefully as she did everything else. Chris waited for the claim stub, joined Megan, and together they entered the club, then followed a hostess out to the back terrace, where a large white tent had been erected. The crowd was thick, spilling onto the terrace. The hum of conversation filled the air, along with the upbeat music of a quartet playing from the far end of the tent.

Before Chris had time to even form the thought that a cocktail would be nice, a waiter appeared before them, bearing champagne. Chris accepted one glass and handed it to Megan, who distractedly smiled her thanks. He could see that she was already inventorying the crowd for the "must greet now" people. This was what he did when he left his kitchen at Paradis for a while each night, except his restaurant was far more intimate in setting and numbers. He accepted a glass of wine for himself and prepared for a whole lot of smiling.

Time—and Megan—marched on. He met the Starworths and gave Leona a personal invitation to visit Paradis. Leona then introduced Megan to their friends, a group that seemed to number in the hundreds. Megan's stamina amazed him. She talked and laughed with everybody, signed everything from posters of herself to cocktail napkins, and had her picture taken so many times that she should have been blinded from the flashes. Finally, Leona stepped in, settling a hand on Megan's arm.

"Please don't feel that you have to entertain all of us," she said to Megan. "After all, that's what the band is for." She gestured over at the dance floor, where couples now moved in slow, romantic embraces. "And the Hammonds have arrived," she added. "I'm sure you'd enjoy some time with them."

Chris quickly scanned the crowd. Matt stood in a small gathering of people, holding court. Ted and Lisa were at his side. His gaze met Ted's, and then Ted looked away.

After Leona had departed, Megan said, "I need to go say hello to Matt. It would look odd if I didn't."

He nodded his agreement.

As they approached the group, Ted's expression changed to one of alarm. Chris raised his brows, telegraphing "what's up?" Ted shook his head in a subtle "no closer" gesture. Chris slowed and reached for Megan, but as always she was moving straight on, intent on her goal. Megan might be a force of nature, but Chris had the feeling she was about to run them smack into a hurricane.

"HELLO, MATT," MEGAN SAID as the group with the Hammonds opened their circle to include Chris and her.

Matt's responding hello was even tighter than usual, but she put that off to the fact that she had Mr.

Persona Non Grata by her side. After introductions were made, her boss lapsed into silence. Trying to fill the gap, she exchanged pleasantries with his acquaintances, then accepted their good wishes for Sunday's race. They'd just moved on to more general talk when Matt cut in.

"Megan, if you wouldn't mind following me outside for a moment?"

The words had been cast in the form of a question, but there was no mistaking them for anything but an order.

"Perhaps your friend could come with you, also?"

Megan wanted to say no, to tell him to cut out this garbage, but because they were in a public place, she said, "Of course we can," and gave her apologies to the other guests.

Though she was sure it killed him, Matt made a smiling effort at unity as they threaded through the crowd and back onto the terrace. Once they were off to the side, all pretense of politeness fell away. His stance grew stiff and hostile, and in the light of the setting sun, his face appeared flushed. Scarily so. Megan almost wished for the return of the man of ice.

"It didn't take you very long, did it?" he snapped at Chris.

"Very long to do what?" Chris asked, sounding genuinely confused.

"You know what you did. Maybe this time it wasn't destroying an engine out of spite, but dragging Hammond Racing's name through the dirt is sabotage all the same."

Chris's posture now echoed his father's. Megan hadn't noted much physical resemblance between the two men until this moment.

"I'm going to be blunt about this," Chris said. "I don't know what the hell you're talking about."

"I'm talking about the phone call I received this evening. Does the name Miranda Carlyle ring a bell?"

Chris glanced over at Megan, obviously remembering she'd mentioned the name that afternoon. She nodded her head.

"I know who the woman is, but I've never spoken to her," he said to his father.

"Bull. How else would she know about our connection and what happened when you were seventeen? I've made damn sure that incident was buried—ancient history. And now she's doing a story on the Hammond dynasty, as she called it." His laugh was bitter. "Some dynasty. A son who destroys the team's chances of winning Daytona the first time he's with them. A son who turns his back on his father—"

"Stop!" Megan cried. "What's the matter with you, bringing this up here?" she asked in a low voice, now that she had his attention. She hitched her head toward the gathering onlookers. "Carlyle won't even have to do the story. You're broadcasting it for her. And if she has been nosing around, that's my fault, and not Chris's. She and I have I guess what you'd call a little personality conflict. I don't like the way she snoops and she doesn't like the way I push back, so she's probably put in some extra hours to get even with me. Bottom line…it's not Chris, okay?"

Hammond turned on her. "I'll give you credit for not backing down from me, Megan. Few do that. But to do so while telling me that you're responsible for my family's impending humiliation? What kind of judgment does that show?" His chest rose and fell with agitation. He drew in a ragged breath and continued his barrage. "It's your fault that he left his island and started this mess," he added, flicking his hand toward Chris in a dismissive gesture. "Business is about balancing cost versus reward. Your cost outweighs any potential reward to Hammond Racing. You're driving Sunday because I can't afford to pull you, but after that, you're done."

Shock at his words quickly gave way to anger. "You have got to be kidding! I might be a rookie, but I'm no idiot. If you even try that, I'll have a team of lawyers on you by Monday morning."

He stepped back as though he'd just received a physical blow. "Don't threaten me!"

"Then don't you threaten me," Megan replied.

"Enough," Chris said in a deep and firm voice. "Megan was right. This isn't the place for this discussion, if you can call it that."

And it wasn't any place Megan wanted to be.

"Let's go," she urged Chris.

"We will," he replied. "Soon. But first we have to do a little damage control. Matt—Dad—go back in the tent and rejoin your guests. Get a smile on your face, or at least don't look as though you'd like to call down a barbarian horde. Talk, laugh, make the rounds once, and then leave.

"Megan and I will be at your office at eight tomorrow. I expect you and Ted to be there. We're going to have a talk somewhere far from prying eyes and ears and get this matter settled. Is that clear?"

Matt didn't look diminished to Megan quite so much as he looked hollow. The color had drained from his face, and his military posture had slumped into something less rigid. While he didn't answer his son, he did turn and head back to the tent.

"Are you okay?" Chris asked her.

"Probably as okay as I'm going to be," she said. Now that the hostilities had died down, she felt tears coming on and knew she couldn't hold them back. "Chris, I can't go back in there."

"Come with me," Chris said.

He wished he could sweep her back to Bequia, where life was simpler and the problems not so serious. But he couldn't. Not now, and not until she had fulfilled all of her dreams. But he could bring a little joy back into the evening. He grasped her hand and drew her along with him.

"Where are you taking me?" she asked.

"Not far," he replied as they neared the tent. He paused just long enough to spot his father back with Ted and Lisa. Ted looked his way, and Chris shrugged both as an apology of sorts and to let him know that he'd done all he could. Then he led Megan past the tent and to the edge of the golf course, where he stopped in front of a bench.

"Sit down for a second," he said.

"Why?"

"No questions. Just trust me."

"I do," she replied, and he considered that the second-best gift he could get this evening. As for the very best, he'd know in a couple of minutes.

Megan sat, and Chris squatted down in front of her.

"What are you doing?"she asked.

In answer, he quickly slipped off her red shoes and set them on the bench beside her.

"You said the first chance you got, they were going. So now they're gone." He took her hand. "Come on."

She rose, and he led her so that they were partially obscured from the view of those in the party by a row of tall shrubs. The band had begun playing something slow and jazzy and soothing.

"Dance with me?" he asked.

She tilted her head and looked at him quizzically. "Here? And after all of that?"

"Here, and most definitely after all of that," he affirmed.

She gave a shaky laugh. "I'd totally stopped hearing the music."

"Never a good thing," Chris replied.

And then he took her in his arms. They moved well together, but he already knew that. Still, Megan was restless.

"Relax," he said. "Just feel."

If she gained even a tenth of the comfort he was offering by holding her, she'd soon calm. And so they danced as one song slipped into the next. And when he felt her relax in his arms, he began to talk.

"The summer my mom died was a damn mess," he said. "I was shipped off to live with a father who hadn't known I existed and left daily in the path of Ted and his younger brother, Kurt. It was kind of a law of the jungle thing around the Hammonds. Ted and Kurt viewed me as a threat to their position with their father, and so they started gunning for me."

Megan tipped her head up to meet his eyes. "All I've ever known is Stewie, so I can't imagine that."

"And I'd been an only child, so I was pretty blown away. And they were smart enough to know that I'd never go to our father. I was one ticked-off kid. It wasn't so much that Matt was bad. He just wasn't the dead heroic fireman, you know?" He shook his head. "Wow, that sounds so insane as an adult, but when I was seventeen…"

"I know. I remember those days."

He hugged her closer and said, "It's good to have

you back. To be able to say the crazy stuff and know you won't judge me. Anyway, when their terror campaign didn't dislodge me, Ted and Kurt pulled out the real ammo. They trashed an engine at Hammond Racing and made it look as though I'd done it. Our father didn't even ask me if I'd been responsible. He just assumed. And I was so ticked and hurt and resentful that I never bothered to correct him. If Ted and Kurt wanted the guy, they could have him."

The music had stopped, but he wasn't ready to let go of Megan. She didn't seem to be letting go of him, either.

"All I wanted to do was get back to Miami, where my aunt and cousin were living. Susan, my dad's secretary, was the only person who'd been nice to me. I went to her and asked her to lend me money for a bus ticket. Instead, she drove me home herself, and told my father that I had wanted to be back with my mother's family. I never heard directly from him again. The next summer, when I graduated from high school, I got a graduation card. It was unsigned, and in it was a check that would have covered four years of college and some document I was supposed to sign agreeing that the money was to be used for a four-year college program and nothing else. He knew from Susan that I planned to attend a culinary institute. I mailed the check back and made my own way."

Megan went up on tiptoe and brushed a kiss

against his mouth. "I'm sorry you had to go through all of that."

He chuckled. "For a while there, I was sorry, too. I was the most miserable jerk who ever worked a grill line. Then it occurred to me that I needed to get over myself. And so I pulled it together, and here I am."

"I'm glad that you are, and also I'm sorry for thinking the worst of you the other night. I know you better than that, Chris. It was just my old insecurities. I might be good at racing, but as I'm sure Stewie told you while I was getting ready tonight, I've made some pretty awful mistakes in the boyfriend area."

"He did say something about a few losers and users."

She nodded. "It was more than a few. Some of the stories are funny. Some, not so much. I thought the last guy I dated was perfect. He thought I was the quick route to a job as a fabricator."

Chris hated to hear that she'd been hurt. "I'm betting that he found himself more in a dead end."

"Very dead," Megan agreed. "All the same, I decided to stop dating until I was better at picking up loser and user signals, and also had a clue about balancing work and play. When I met you, I figured even if I was wrong about you in the long run, I'd only be around for the short run, so it didn't matter."

"You've gotten pretty good at the work and play thing. But now, after we've found out that life is better—if maybe a little crazier—when we're together, do you want me around for more than the short run?"

"I do, but—"

He silenced her with a kiss. "Forget the problems. Those we'll deal with tomorrow. For now, all I want you to know is that I love you, and this time around, I'm holding on."

"You love me?"

"Pretty much since the day you walked into Paradis, I knew you were the one. I might have been temporarily stopped by the idea of having to deal with my father once I found out about that little issue. All the same, I knew you were it for me." The music had started again, and he smiled at the perfect timing.

"But—"

He kissed her again. "Just dance. That's all you need to do. I don't need the words back, and we don't need to solve the world's problems tonight. I just wanted you to know."

And so they danced.

"This time around," Megan murmured.

"What about it?"

"I can't believe you used those words—this time around."

"What do you mean?"

"I have this thing I say in my head—almost a mantra—before the start of a race. I tell myself, this time around I'll do it better, faster, smarter."

"Well," he said, "I don't know if we could do it any faster than the first time around, but I think after tomorrow, once we've settled things with my father, we'll have the better and smarter part taken care of."

"Good," she said. "Because I love you."

And now he had the very best gift he could get tonight.

She twined her arms around his neck and added, "With all my heart."

What else could he do but kiss her again? He pulled her close and was about to make good on the thought when he heard his name being yelled. He turned to see Ted running toward them.

"I've been looking everywhere for you," he said, winded. "It's Dad. He's in the clubhouse. An ambulance is on its way."

CHAPTER SEVEN

THERE WAS A LOT TO be said for hospitals bigger than a city block, filled with experts. By ten o'clock the next morning, Chris's father had been moved to a private room and was as irritable as a caged wolverine. He was annoying the nurses, driving Susan to distraction and demanding to read his test results himself. Chris, who'd stayed with Ted all night in the waiting room, drinking bad coffee and watching worse television, couldn't have been happier to see his father bounce back.

Outside his dad's room, he glanced at his watch, then said to his brother, "I should go shower. I have a business meeting coming up."

"Local business?" Ted asked.

Chris nodded. "Relatively. I've decided to open a place in Miami. A guy I know owns a resort on South Beach, and…" He shrugged. "Let's just say I could use a base on the mainland."

Ted smiled. "I take it you plan to be here more?"

"As much as possible."

"Looks like we Hammonds have a good reason

to work on our interpersonal communication, or at least get some, don't you think?"

"Agreed, but right now, I have to go get ready."

"Can you give me a minute?" Ted hitched a thumb toward their father's room. "Speaking of family conversations, I've got something I need to say to him, and I'd like you to be there when I do."

Chris knew his brother was referring to the engine sabotage of yore. "Hey, man, that was light-years ago. Dad and I will work it out, regardless."

Ted's smile was crooked. "It's either this, or you take that swing at me I promised you."

Chris laughed. "We're in the right place for some first aid, but I'm not going to do that, either."

"Okay, but the bottom line is that I'm going talk to Dad whether or not you're there, so you might as well come along," Ted replied, then went into Matt's room.

Figuring Ted was right, Chris followed.

"What are you doing here?" his father asked, looking over the tops of his reading glasses.

"Same thing I've been doing since they brought you in…waiting to be sure you're okay," Chris replied.

"That was good of you, all things considered."

And that, Chris supposed, was a Matt Hammond apology.

"Did you bring coffee?" his father asked.

"You're not allowed to have coffee," Chris pointed out.

Matt shook out the newspaper's financial section and began reading again. Chris bit back a laugh at the dismissal. It might have carried a little more gravitas if his father weren't wearing a baby blue hospital gown.

"So, I take it you're feeling better, Dad?" Chris asked.

"They should discharge me. They're wasting my time."

"Your cardiologist says tomorrow afternoon," Ted reminded their father. "And if you're feeling up to it, you can watch the race from the war room on Sunday."

Matt snorted, but kept reading the paper. "The war room. I'll watch the race from the viewing stand, same as always."

"We'll see," Ted said in a judicious tone.

"And in the meantime, while you're here they'll send you all the interns you could ever want to scare," Chris offered by way of amusement.

His father refolded the paper and settled it in his lap. "They wouldn't dare have an intern poke and prod at me. And if you two are going to be in here, pull up chairs. I feel like a corpse at a wake with you standing there like that."

This time, Chris did laugh, and he and Ted pulled up chairs.

"Dad, I've got something I have to tell you," Ted announced.

"I don't like conversations that start this way," Matt said.

"You probably won't like the rest much, either, but it's long overdue," Ted replied.

Matt frowned. "Let's hear it."

"You know when that engine got trashed? The one that Miranda Carlyle has decided is the scoop of the century?"

"Of course. I expect to be turning down yet another request for an interview from Carlyle as soon as I'm out of here. What about it?"

"It would be a pretty incomplete interview, if you gave one. You don't know the full story."

"Doesn't matter. It's in the past," Matt said. "It's time the Hammonds move on…myself included."

"The problem is that this Hammond can't move on until he's told you that Chris had nothing to do with the sabotage," Ted replied. "It was my fault. Mine and Kurt's."

Matt frowned. "You were adults…at least purportedly so. And you stood to gain as much from a good showing at Daytona as I did, so why the hell would you do something like that?"

"I don't know. It seemed…" Ted sighed. "Okay, here it is. You were always picking favorites, pitting Kurt against me, and when Chris was added to the mix, Kurt and I finally had a common adversary. We needed him gone. The best way to do that was to hit you where it hurt most—at Hammond Racing."

"I'll admit I was more attentive to work and less so to my children over the years, but this is too dog-eat-dog, even for a Hammond. You set up a boy?"

"I'm not proud of it. And I've apologized to Chris."

Ted looked for confirmation to Chris, who nodded.

"I'm square with him," he told Matt. "And I'm not emotionally scarred for life or anything."

"I should hope not," Matt replied. "Hammonds are made of sterner stuff. But why didn't you tell me what was going on?"

He shrugged. "It's not as though we talked. Ted and Kurt wanted me gone, and I wanted to be gone. You weren't the father I'd grown up believing I had, and I felt like an outsider, anyway."

Matt removed his reading glasses and placed them on the bedside table.

"What your mother did was wrong, not letting me know about you," he said. "No matter that we didn't work out, I would have been there for you. I think I was angry, and I think you might have gotten the brunt of that."

"I know. I didn't get that when I was seventeen, but I figured it out later. She scammed you as much as she did me. That had to hurt. I'm sorry for that."

"It shouldn't have been your issue."

Yet another Matt Hammond apology, but it helped Chris put that past a little more behind him.

"It's done, all of it. The question is where we go from here. And, honestly, I don't know what I want. I can tell you…and you, Ted, that I don't want to be a part of the Hammond empire. I like running my own show. Something, now that I think of it, I probably got from you," he said to his father.

"Fair enough," Matt replied.

"And I can also tell you that I'm going to be with Megan whenever our schedules permit. I don't feel that your permission is required, but a little acceptance would be good. I love her, and I plan to have a life with her. I know this could lead to gossip, and I think the best way to deal with it is to hand them the facts. I'm your son. We didn't know that until I was seventeen. Our relationship now is not the press's business. And I am not and never will be involved in Hammond Racing. Pretty simple stuff."

"Agreed," his father said. "Cut all emotion from it. When you came to Daytona this time, Chris, it was a bolt out of the blue. I reacted out of emotion, which is something I try to avoid. It's bad for business."

"Not to mention your heart rhythm," Ted added, earning a harrumph from his father.

Business would always be Matt's bottom line, and Chris could now accept that and not take it personally.

"So long as Megan performs, she has a place at Hammond Racing, and you can promise her that she'll get no more unprofessional outbursts from me. But just because she's dating you doesn't mean she gets any breaks, either. I'd like you to tell her all of that, as I assume you'll be seeing her before they let me out of this overpriced prison."

Chris laughed. "I'll let her know. And I'm sure she'll stick around…unless a better offer comes up."

Matt scowled. "That's no way to talk to a sick man. And about that, did Ted tell you what's going on?"

"I knew already. Susan has always given me updates."

"I have to remember to fire her one day," his father muttered, but even if he hadn't ended the words with a quick smile, Chris would have known he didn't mean it.

"I'm a damn healthy man for having a failing heart. So long as my numbers stay good, I'm on the transplant list. And as of this last round of tests, it's still a go. I'm going to cut back on the emotion over things I can't control and hope for the best." He smiled a rare, genuine smile. "I'll make sure this next heart has a little more room for my kids, okay? Now you two get out of here and let me get back to my paper."

Chris didn't know where he and his dad would end up, but he'd take this for a starting line.

RACE DAY. THERE WAS no feeling like it!

Megan woke and stretched, briefly touching her

hand to her necklace and thinking of Chris. Between his dad, his final meeting with Hal, and her crazy schedule, they hadn't been able to see each other. He promised, though, that after the race he'd be waiting for her. All the more reason to go fast.

She smiled at the sounds of Stewart doing his thing in the galley.

"Aren't you going to ask me what flavor of smoothie?" she called through the door to him.

"Smoothie? I wouldn't make you that travesty of a breakfast, especially on Valentine's Day."

"Chris!"

Megan bounded from her bed, threw open the door and flung herself at him.

Laughing, he caught her. "Morning, champ! You're looking adorable. The best advertising a guy could have."

She glanced down and realized she was wearing a Paradis server's shirt that she'd wheedled out of him back on Bequia.

"Like it?"

He kissed her. "I like the contents a whole lot better."

"So what do I get for breakfast?" she asked, trying to peek around him at the galley.

"*We* get omelets, papaya, mango and bananas broiled with brown sugar."

She sighed her pleasure. "After Stewart starts grad school, I'm hiring you."

He laughed. "You couldn't afford me, but once it's open, you can feel free to stop in at the new place in South Beach anytime you want. I might even comp your meal."

"Big spender," she teased. "So you're doing the deal for sure?"

He nodded. "I am. Hal and I ironed out the final details late last night. Monday it goes into the hands of our lawyers."

"This is *so* cool!"

"I can go cooler, yet," he said, pulling a small, square box from his pocket. "Happy Valentine's Day, Megan."

She looked around her home on wheels as though a gift shop might suddenly materialize. "But I don't have anything to give you."

He smiled, holding out the box. "I have you. What more could I want? Now open it, champ."

She took the silver-colored box and opened the lid. Inside was nestled a small and beautifully detailed, gold version of a NASCAR race car.

"Chris, it's beautiful!"

"I thought we could put it on the chain with your coral charm—both parts of your life brought together, just as we're going to be."

She smiled, but tears still welled. She had never known that happiness ran so deeply. "Thank you. This is the most wonderful gift I've ever received."

"Then turn around, and let's get this together."

She did as Chris directed, and in no time he'd added the car to her necklace.

"Done," he decreed.

She turned around, intent on giving him another kiss, but he fended her off.

"Uh-uh. I don't think you want to start that now, not when we've got another party with a seven-thirty breakfast reservation."

She looked around. "Reservation? Here?"

"We are about to be joined by my dad, who has decided to come and make peace, which means you're seriously underdressed." Chris planted his hands on her shoulders and turned her toward the bedroom. "Get moving, champ. You have the day of a lifetime ahead of you."

She danced out of his grip.

"I'm not so sure *this* is the day," she said. "I can think of far better days to come."

Love and laughter and joy and big NASCAR wins shimmered on the horizon. No doubt about it. This time around, they'd done it just right.

* * * * *

REQUEST YOUR FREE BOOKS!

2 FREE NOVELS
FROM THE ROMANCE COLLECTION
PLUS 2 FREE GIFTS!

YES! Please send me 2 FREE novels from the Romance Collection and my 2 FREE gifts (gifts are worth about $10). After receiving them, if I don't wish to receive any more books, I can return the shipping statement marked "cancel." If I don't cancel, I will receive 4 brand-new novels every month and be billed just $5.74 per book in the U.S. or $6.24 per book in Canada. That's a saving of at least 28% off the cover price. It's quite a bargain! Shipping and handling is just 50¢ per book in the U.S. and 75¢ per book in Canada.* I understand that accepting the 2 free books and gifts places me under no obligation to buy anything. I can always return a shipment and cancel at any time. Even if I never buy another book, the two free books and gifts are mine to keep forever.

194 MDN E4LY   394 MDN E4MC

Name	(PLEASE PRINT)

Address	Apt. #

City	State/Prov.	Zip/Postal Code

Signature (if under 18, a parent or guardian must sign)

Mail to **The Reader Service:**
IN U.S.A.: P.O. Box 1867, Buffalo, NY 14240-1867
IN CANADA: P.O. Box 609, Fort Erie, Ontario L2A 5X3

Not valid for current subscribers to the Romance Collection
or the Romance/Suspense Collection.

Want to try two free books from another line?
Call 1-800-873-8635 or visit www.morefreebooks.com.

* Terms and prices subject to change without notice. Prices do not include applicable taxes. N.Y. residents add applicable sales tax. Canadian residents will be charged applicable provincial taxes and GST. Offer not valid in Quebec. This offer is limited to one order per household. All orders subject to approval. Credit or debit balances in a customer's account(s) may be offset by any other outstanding balance owed by or to the customer. Please allow 4 to 6 weeks for delivery. Offer available while quantities last.

Your Privacy: Harlequin Books is committed to protecting your privacy. Our Privacy Policy is available online at www.eHarlequin.com or upon request from the Reader Service. From time to time we make our lists of customers available to reputable third parties who have a product or service of interest to you. If you would prefer we not share your name and address, please check here. ☐

Help us get it right—We strive for accurate, respectful and relevant communications. To clarify or modify your communication preferences, visit us at www.ReaderService.com/consumerschoice.

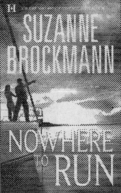

Things aren't always as they seem....

Acclaimed author

DONNA BIRDSELL

When young widow
Dannie Treat discovers
a bag full of money in her
garage, she thinks her prayers
have been answered. The
insurance company has refused
to pay on her husband's death
policy because there is no
body, and she's having trouble
supporting her four young
children on her paycheck as a
preschool teacher. But when
she discovers the money is
counterfeit, she begins to
wonder if her husband's death
was really no accident after all.

A Widow in Paradise

In stores today wherever trade paperback books are sold!

Free bonus book in this volume!
Suburban Secrets
by Donna Birdsell
Truth or Dare: It's not just for slumber parties anymore

www.eHarlequin.com

PHDB739